BLACKSTONE RANGER HERO

Blackstone Ranger Book 3

ALICIA MONTGOMERY

Also by Alicia Montgomery

The True Mates Series

Fated Mates

Blood Moon

Romancing the Alpha

Witch's Mate

Taming the Beast

Tempted by the Wolf

The Lone Wolf Defenders Series

Killian's Secret

Loving Quinn

All for Connor

The True Mates Standalone Novels

Holly Jolly Lycan Christmas

A Mate for Jackson: Bad Alpha Dads

True Mates Generations

A Twist of Fate

Claiming the Alpha

Alpha Ascending

A Witch in Time

Highland Wolf

Daughter of the Dragon

Shadow Wolf

A Touch of Magic

Heart of the Wolf

The Blackstone Mountain Series

The Blackstone Dragon Heir

The Blackstone Bad Dragon

The Blackstone Bear

The Blackstone Wolf

The Blackstone Lion

The Blackstone She-Wolf

The Blackstone She-Bear

The Blackstone She-Dragon

Blackstone Rangers Series

Blackstone Ranger Chief

Blackstone Ranger Charmer

Blackstone Ranger Hero

Blackstone Ranger Rogue

Blackstone Ranger Guardian

This is a work of fiction. Names, characters, businesses, places, events, locales, and incidents are either the products of the author's imagination or used in a fictitious manner. Any resemblance to actual persons, living or dead, or actual events is purely coincidental.

www.aliciamontgomeryauthor.com
First Electronic publication September 2020

Edited by LaVerne Clark
Cover by Jacqueline Sweet
091620

About the Author

Alicia Montgomery has always dreamed of becoming a romance novel writer. She started writing down her stories in now long-forgotten diaries and notebooks, never thinking that her dream would come true. After taking the well-worn path to a stable career, she is now plunging into the world of self-publishing.

facebook.com/aliciamontgomeryauthor
twitter.com/amontromance
bookbub.com/authors/alicia-montgomery

Chapter 1

"C'mon, Rogers, don't be such a pussy!"

Daniel Rogers breathed a sigh and took a sip of his beer. "I think you guys are doing just fine without me," he shouted over the loud din of the music pumping through the speakers.

Anders Stevens rolled his eyes. "Seriously? You're not going to join us? Not even one lousy dollar for those hardworking girls up there?"

He lifted his head an inch, forcing himself to look at the three scantily-clad women on stage. One of them, wearing only sparkly nipple covers and a G-string, hung upside down from a pole. "They certainly are ... talented."

"Yeah, very *big* talents," Anders added with a waggle of his eyebrows. "Look, the groom-to-be and Russel"—he jerked a thumb at the back of the room to where their two other companions, Damon Cooper and Gabriel Russel, were huddled by the buffet table—"aren't going to be participating in the festivities anytime soon, so why don't you just come up here? There's three of them and two of us, so I think we can make the equation work."

"Hey!" a feminine voice protested. "What am I? Chopped liver?"

Anders turned to their third compatriot, J.D. McNamara, the only female in their group. Though technically this was Damon's bachelor party, one of the groom's conditions was they include one of his best friends since childhood, even if she was a girl.

Currently, J.D. was waving dollar bills at the stripper on the pole. "I know you enjoy the show, McNamara, but I didn't think you played for our team. Or are you thinking of taking me up on my offer?" he said with a glint in his eyes.

J.D. rolled her eyes. "If Rogers doesn't want to participate in the fun, you don't have to rag on him. I mean, these poor, hardworking girls could probably use the tips. Do you know Destiny"—she nodded at the brunette on the left side—"is almost done with her nursing degree? If you could spare her those dollar bills in your pocket, Anders, she could maybe afford her textbooks next semester."

"Those ain't dollar bills, sweetheart," he said with an impish smile.

Daniel sighed once again and pulled his wallet out of his pocket, taking out half the bills and handing them to J.D. "Here, for Destiny's textbooks," he said before getting up from his chair.

"Giving up already?" Anders called.

"Jeez, stop acting like those clingy girls you kick outta your bed, Stevens. I gotta go to the john, all right?" Turning toward the exit, he walked out of the private VIP area and into the main room of the Pink Palace Gentlemen's Club.

Of course, the outside was not much better than the private party rooms, if anything, they were worse. Though it was a "gentlemen's club," there was nothing very gentlemanly about the garish pink, red, and black decor, neon lights, or the various scantily-clad women onstage and the loud, jeering men who cheered them on.

Daniel was no prude, but he just wasn't raised this way. Though he got ribbed a lot because he was polite and nice to everyone—men and women—he didn't pay any mind to the criticisms. A gentleman—a real one—treated everyone else better than they would treat themselves, at least that's what Pops always said. Beau Rogers was old-fashioned in that way and taught his only son the same set of rules he'd followed his whole life.

He wouldn't normally have gone to this place, or even to Las Vegas, except that it was one of his good friend's bachelor party. Pops also said that loyalty to one's friends was important, so Daniel felt obliged to come to this weekend getaway, especially since Damon's circle of friends was tiny. Actually, as far as he knew, it only consisted of the people who came to Vegas.

The four men had gone through the Blackstone Rangers training program together and a kind of bond had forged between them. Daniel admired Damon, who had risen up to the position of chief. Though Daniel himself had been eyeing the promotion, he knew Damon deserved it—he was a natural leader, and everyone looked up to him. Besides, there was a lot of responsibility that came with being chief, and he didn't envy the long hours, paperwork, and the bureaucracy that Damon had to deal with. Nope, he was fine being a ranger, as he had been the last five years.

Joining the Blackstone Rangers seemed like the natural career for Daniel. For one thing, his inner grizzly bear loved the outdoors, and the job allowed him to spend most of the day roaming the forests and mountains. And of course, it was in his blood. Before retiring to Texas on his ranch, Beau had been a ranger for over forty years. It had done his old man proud when he decided to join after graduating from college with his forestry degree.

Daniel made his way to the men's room, did his business, and then exited. He was walking down the dark hallway that led back to the main room when he saw two shadowy figures ahead.

"Please ... sir, you can't—" a pleading voice cried.

"I'll do whatever the fuck I want," came the gruff reply. "I'm a paying customer."

Daniel's hackles rose and his inner grizzly let out a guttural sound. His protective instincts were sounding an alarm, and he strode toward the two figures. "Excuse me," he said. "Is he bothering you, miss?"

His shifter vision immediately adjusted despite the darkness, and the larger of the two figures—male, of course, stinking of cheap cologne and liquor—whirled around to face him. "Wha—who the fuck are you?"

Ignoring the man, he looked to the woman pressed up against the wall. Much like many of the girls here, she was scantily-clad, and her face was caked with makeup, but the wide, frightened look in her eyes made her seem much younger. "S-sir, you should go back to the main floor." The tension and fear rolled off her in waves.

The man's face turned up into an evil grin. "See? Me and Candy here are conducting business. And you should mind your own."

Daniel huffed. "See, normally I do mind my business. But you know what I hate the most?"

"What?"

"I hate bullies." He unleashed the barely controlled anger within him, grabbing the man by the collar, and slamming him up against the wall. Candy let out a squeak and turned, dashing away from them.

The man struggled, but it was no use. Daniel's shifter strength allowed him to lift the man off the ground. Opening his mouth wide, he bared his teeth, letting his incisors grow out, his eyes glowing with the presence of his inner bear.

"What the—" His eyes went wide. "You're one of them!"

He let out an inhuman growl, then dropped the man, who crumpled to the ground. "You bet," he said, looking at the pathetic man in disgust. "Now get the fuck out of here. If I see you approach any woman here—I'm going to hunt you down and make you regret it." Not bothering to look back at the man, he marched out.

By the time he entered the private room again, he and his bear had sufficiently calmed down. In fact, the mask of calm he put on his face belied his earlier rage. He hated losing his temper, but he also couldn't stand it when strong people took advantage of weaker ones. And just because the young woman chose to work at a strip club didn't mean she was fair game.

"You all right?" Gabriel asked as he came over to the buffet to pile a plate high with food.

"Yeah, I'm fine. How's the groom?" he asked, looking slyly over at Damon. The chief's back was turned to them as he hunched over while fiddling on his phone. "Does he feel as miserable as he looks?"

Gabriel guffawed. "What do you think?"

According to Gabriel, Damon had been strong-armed into this outing, as he didn't want to be away from his mate and future wife, Anna Victoria. Daniel could understand, even though he didn't have a mate himself. His parents were fated mates, so he knew how special that could be. Damon would not only have no interest in any other woman around, but it would also pain him to be away from her. "Remind me again why we're here?"

The lion shifter huffed. "I owe Anders a huge favor, okay?

I'll tell you more some other time. But right now, keep him distracted so he doesn't shit on either Damon or me. I promise, this will all be over soon."

Daniel knew the "secret" plan of course, which was one of the reasons he'd consented to come here in the first place. "All right." Taking his plate of food, he wandered back to the mini-stage in the center of the room and sat down next to J.D., munching on wings, pizza, and french fries.

About fifteen minutes later, the DJ's booming voice interrupted the playing music over the speakers. "And now we have some special entertainment just for the groom," the disembodied voice of the DJ announced.

The strippers all stopped dancing, picked up their cash from the floor, and disappeared through the curtains at the rear of the stage.

"Hey!" Anders protested as he waved a fistful of bills. "Where are you going?"

"Anders, c'mon," J.D. said as she jumped to her feet. "Let's go to the main room."

"Main room? But we were having fun in here," Anders complained.

Daniel followed J.D.'s lead. "Sounds like a plan."

J.D. hooked her arm around the tiger shifter's. "Dude, I think I saw a bachelorette party out there. Bet they're a lot of fun. And looking for some company."

"Really?" Anders's face lit up. "Well then, what are we waiting for? You can be my wing woman, McNamara."

J.D rolled her eyes as she led him out of there, Daniel right behind them. As he followed the two, he couldn't help but feel like someone was watching him. Turning his head, he looked around, but there were too many people around them to pinpoint anyone looking at him. His grizzly seethed, yowling at him to investigate. Normally, he would have followed his bear's instinct, but they were in a strip club, not deep in the mountains. So instead, he sat next to J.D. at their new table, which was right by the stage.

"Yeah, baby," Anders exclaimed. "Right by the action." He glanced around and saw the group of women at the table next to them, which, based on the crowns and sashes they wore, was the aforementioned bachelorette party. "All right! this is better than being trapped inside with those tight-asses anyway. Hey, baby!" he hollered to one of the women. "Nice tats. They're a piece of art, and so are you. Want me to nail you to the wall?"

J.D. rolled her eyes. "Cut it out, Anders," she said. "They're tryin' to have a good time. Besides, they're not the entertainment." She grabbed his ear and tilted his head toward the stage. "That's what we're here for." She sent an apologetic look to the women.

The lights dimmed as a slow, sensuous beat filled the room. A woman wearing a feather boa entered the stage, and everyone clapped and cheered. With another deep sigh, Daniel settled back, arms folding over his chest. *When was this going to end?* Neither J.D. nor Anders seemed keen on stopping any time soon. He glanced back toward the private room where he guessed Damon was finally enjoying his bachelor party. After all, Gabriel did secretly fly Anna Victoria all the way here. And the lion shifter was nowhere to be seen, which meant he probably snuck out. *Lucky bastard.*

"Sir?"

"Huh?" Whipping around, he saw one of the cocktail waitresses leaning toward him, drink in hand. "This is for you."

He glanced down at the drink. It looked innocuous enough; it even had a cherry in it. "I didn't order this."

"One of the girls sent it over," she said. "Candy. She says it's a thank you gift for earlier."

"Oh." It was a nice gesture, but he really didn't need it. "Um, can you take it back? Or I could pay for it."

"Oh no." She shook her head. "Please, I couldn't." Before he could protest, she turned on her heel and walked away.

Glancing at the drink, he took a sniff. It smelled like gin and tonic, the flowery bouquet of the liquor tickling his nostrils. However, there was something about it—

A movement caught his eye from the corner of his vision. While everyone had their attention on the stage, someone at the table next to them stood up. He didn't know why, but he just had to look at who it was.

It was one of the females from the bachelorette party. She walked around her friends with an unsteady gait, grabbing onto the back of a chair to steady herself. When she did, she proceeded forward and something about the way she moved made it difficult to tear his eyes away from her.

He took a nervous sip of the drink in his hand, barely tasting the alcohol. His hand trembled as he pulled the glass away from his lips, but his gaze never left her.

The world around him slowed down, his focus pinpointing on the woman. Continuing forward, she came close to their table, but stumbled forward.

He lunged toward her, grabbing one of her arms before she could hit the ground. She let out a yelp as he pulled her upright, a dark curtain of hair covering her face.

"Are you okay, miss?" Thanks to his shifter reflexes, he didn't even spill the drink in his right hand.

Wobbling on her feet, she brushed the hair from her face. "Yeah, I'm good. Did you—" She stopped as their eyes met. Velvety brown eyes, the color of milk chocolate, widened in surprise.

Mine.

Jesus!

After that, he couldn't quite describe what happened next—it was kind of like being punched in the gut. But in a good way, if there was such a thing. His bear roared from within him, its massive paws beating at the ground. They had found their *mate.*

"Sorry about that," she said. "Too much to drink ... normally I can handle it but ... special occasion, you know?"

"Special occasion," he echoed.

"Well, uh, thanks for the catch," she slurred as she patted him on the arm. "Whoa ... you must work out. Your biceps are like rocks." She gave them a firm squeeze, which made blood rush out of his head and down to ... well, his *other* head. "Er, thanks again."

He watched her pivot on her heel and walk away from him, unable to move or say anything. The room seemed to have quieted down, and the only thing he could hear was the pounding of his heart in his chest.

His inner grizzly, however, roared at him and slammed its paws at his insides as if saying, *go after her, you idiot!*

"Shit!" He snapped out of it. *I have to go after her!* She was their mate. But what would he say? Or do? Or how could he explain? Based on her lack of animal, she was obviously human.

Panic rose in him as his bear paced back and forth, probably wishing it could talk. *What would Pops say?* But his mind went blank. *Crap!*

His hand gripped around the glass he was still holding. *C'mon, Rogers, think.* Raising the glass to his lips, he downed the entire drink without another thought. The alcohol ran smoothly down his throat, warming his insides.

I should just go after her. His bear agreed, nodding its block head. Slamming the glass down on the table, he strode toward the direction of the restrooms.

Whoa.

A wave of dizziness hit him as he made his way to the back

of the room. As a shifter, alcohol didn't stay in his system very long, and it took a lot to get him drunk. Did he drink too fast? Or was there something—

His bear growled for attention as it pointed its snout forward. *There she was*, it seemed to say excitedly. Quickly, he caught up to her before she entered the ladies' room and blocked the door.

"What the hell—oh!" she exclaimed. "It's you."

"Yeah," he said. "It's me ..." Why the heck did his tongue feel like it was going numb?

She straightened her shoulders, and planted her hands on her hips. "Can I help you?"

If she said anything after that, he wasn't sure. He couldn't stop staring at her—his mate was gorgeous. Her long, dark hair reminded him of those chocolate commercials where they swirled the dark liquid with caramel. She was wearing a sleeveless dress that showed off her tawny skin and an intricate tattoo of what appeared to be a stained glass window on her upper arm. And her body ... *damn*. Curves everywhere. It made him want to get on his knees and thank whoever up there deemed him worthy enough to have this goddess as his mate.

"Hello?" She waved a hand at him. "Dude, are you okay?"

"I am now," he said dreamily. "Now that you're here."

She rolled her eyes. "Uh-huh. What do you want?"

You. Only you from now on.

Her eyes went wide. "Excuse me?"

Crap. He said that out loud. "I mean, uh ..." God, why the hell was his brain so foggy? Was that an effect of meeting his mate? "I just ... wanted to make sure you were okay. You seemed to be unsteady on your feet."

"Yeah, five vodka cranberries will do that to you," she said sheepishly.

"I know," he lurched forward, backing her up to the other

side, pressing her against the wall. He braced himself with his forearms before he crushed her fully. *Shit, shit, shit!*

"Oh." She didn't protest though, or push him off. In fact, if he didn't know any better, he swore he saw the glitter of desire in her eyes and smell her arousal. "So," she said, her voice low and throaty. "Do you think ... maybe we should, uh, get out of here? Find some fun of our own?"

"I'll follow you to the end of the world if you ask me to, baby doll."

Maybe it was the throbbing in his head. Or maybe it was the sun streaming in through his lids. Whatever it was that woke him, Daniel only knew that when he opened his eyes, a dreaded feeling filled his chest. It was like his stomach was filled with ice, and he didn't want to get up.

What the fuck happened last night?

He blinked and took a deep breath. "Ugh." His mouth tasted like shit. Groggily, he pushed himself up and—

"Where the fuck am I?"

It looked like a low-rent motel room, based on the cheap, worn furniture, the outdated decor and springy mattress underneath him. This was definitely not their suite at the Aria.

Slinking out of bed, he rubbed his aching temple. Glancing down, he realized he was shirtless, but still wearing last night's jeans and socks, though his belt buckle was undone. An image flashed in his mind.

Red painted fingernails reaching for the buckle.

Yellow, blue, and red ink on warm tawny skin.

Pouty lips. Velvet brown eyes turning dark with desire.

Thick lashes lowering.

And—

Nothing.

A big, fat blank.

He sank back down on the bed and buried his face in his hands. Why did he feel like something was wrong? Like something was missing.

Christ, what did I have to drink?

As he tried to retrace his steps, a different, dreaded feeling came over him. *That drink.* It was the last thing he remembered consuming. Was it drugged? He didn't doubt it. He should have burned off the alcohol in one gin and tonic in minutes. When he came out of the private room, his bear had been telling him something was wrong.

His inner grizzly roared, then tumbled over, covering its face with its paws. For something to affect even his inner animal, it had to be bad. Bloodsbane, maybe? It was the only substance shifters knew to avoid. But who the hell would—

A loud, insistent ringing pierced into his skull and knocked him out of his thoughts. Scrambling around, he found his phone under the bed. Grabbing it, he quickly answered. "Hello?" Ow. Even talking made his head hurt.

"Rogers, where the hell are you?" came Anders's furious voice over the receiver.

"I ... uh, I'm not sure."

"Well, wherever the hell you are, you better get your ass to the airport or we'll leave without you."

"What? What time—shit!" he cursed when he glanced up at the clock by the bedside. The digital display showed that it was four in the afternoon. "Damn it ... I'll get there as soon as I can." He spied his shirt hanging from the corner of the bed and grabbed it.

"How long?"

"Just ... wait for me, okay?" *Fuck, fuck, fuck!* "I'm gonna get into a cab now."

After putting his shirt on and checking he still had his wallet in his pocket, Daniel practically flew out of the room. Maybe it was the adrenaline or the panic, but his system was starting to clear up as he made his way down the concrete stairs two at a time. Dashing out of the motel parking lot, he flagged the first cab he saw. "Airport," he barked at the cabbie.

As he sank back into the seat, he swallowed a big gulp of air. The pain in his head was easing, but try as he might, he couldn't put together the events of last night after they had left the private room. Bits and pieces, maybe, but he wasn't sure what was real and what was a dream. The only thing he was sure of was the pit in his stomach was starting to feel like the Grand Canyon as the cab drove further away from the motel.

Think, Rogers. Think.

What happened last night? Where did he go?

Pink Palace. Private Room. Then the main room.

A drink. Someone sent him a drink. *Candy.*

His instincts told him it couldn't have been her.

Maybe it was the guy that was hitting on her. He knew Daniel was a shifter, could feel the animosity from him. Being Vegas, he didn't doubt it would be easy enough to obtain the right drugs to get a shifter intoxicated. *Bloodsbane, most likely.* Every shifter was taught about that stuff.

Surely nothing bad happened. His clothes were still on, his wallet was intact, albeit much lighter, and he didn't seem to have any injuries. All he could remember was a sweet, delicate scent and something soft in his arms. Could he have been with a wo—

"We're here," the cabbie announced.

"Thanks." He tossed the guy a bill. "Keep the change."

As he made his way toward the private jet terminal, he pushed all thoughts aside from his mind. Damon would kill him if he missed his flight home and failed to show up for work tomorrow. The chief already had a lot on his mind, and he didn't want his friend to worry, especially with his wedding less than a week away.

He'd have to forget about what happened last night. Of course, that wouldn't be difficult seeing as he couldn't remember anything anyway.

Chapter 2

Sarah Mendez hung up her apron inside her locker and sat back on the bench behind her, easing her foot out of her shoe. "Ahh," she sighed with relief, propping her heel on her knees and massaging it with her fingers. Working twelve hours overnight on her feet was a killer, but the tips she got working as a waitress at The Griffin Resort and Casino in Las Vegas more than made up for the pain, especially when she got a chance to work the private rooms where the whales played. Once, when a particular frequent guest won big at a hand of Pai Gao, the tip she got paid for nearly a month's rent.

However, she knew that working twelve-hour days and nights wasn't a longtime career move. No, she was going to get out of this particular game, while she could still walk on heels. And today was the day she would make that happen.

Grabbing her towel, she went to the showers and scrubbed off all her makeup and hair products under the hot spray, then toweled off. After changing into a prim, long-sleeved blouse, skirt, and suit jacket, she blow-dried her thick locks and put it up in a sleek bun, then applied the bare minimum of makeup.

When she looked up at the mirror, she startled even herself.

Gone was the sexy, scantily-clad, tattooed, fully made-up cocktail waitress who hustled day and night. In her place was a responsible, straight-laced businesswoman.

Well, not yet. *But you will be, after today,* she told the reflection confidently. Yes, she had a date with destiny.

Okay, so actually, it was a date with her business loan officer down at the National Bank branch on Peach Street, but it was the same thing. After two years of working her ass off on her online business, she was ready to take the plunge and open her own boutique. She already had the perfect location in the affluent downtown Summerlin area, and the leasing company was just waiting for her signature and down payment. The contractor she'd hired was the boyfriend of a regular client and would give her a deal on the renovations. Now, the only thing she needed was the capital.

"Today's the big day, huh?" Cathy, one of her good friends at work, said as she stopped by on her way to the shower room.

"Yup," she said.

"Oh, honey, I'm so happy for you." Cathy embraced her. "You deserve this. You're so talented and smart. I knew you'd be able to get out of here."

"Yeah," Thea, another of the girls, piped in, giving her a playful pinch on the butt. "And you're going to do it all by yourself, without having to rely on a man marrying you."

"Hey now," Cathy warned. "Keep talking like that, and people will think you're all bitter over Stephanie getting married to her rancher from Wyoming."

Thea rolled her eyes. "The only thing I'm bitter about is that since the wedding, he and his big wallet haven't been back."

"Now, ladies," Sarah began, stepping between the two. "Green isn't a good look for any of us."

All three women looked at each other and burst out laughing. *Oh God, I'm going to miss these girls.* They all liked to joke around and pretend to be catty, but they'd saved her sanity during the last five years working here. Truly, they were all happy that Stephanie—the sweetest and kindest person Sarah knew besides her own sister Darcey—had bagged a rich, older man who worshipped the ground she walked on and put a ring on her finger. They had gotten married a few weeks back, and Stephanie quit her job and moved to Wyoming to be with him.

"Our foursome was down to three and now it's going to be just us," Cathy said. "Are you and me gonna grow old together here, Thea?"

The other woman snorted. "Speak for yourself, I'm going to bag myself a whale too. And when we do *my* bachelorette party, we're gonna do it at a male strip club."

Cathy chortled. "That was sneaky of you, Sarah," she said. "Promising the bride you weren't going to take her to a male strip club, but taking her to a female one."

"To be honest, I never had such a good time," Thea added with a chuckle. "Who knew watching men salivating over women and showering them with money could feel so empowering?"

Sarah pasted a smile on her face at the mention of the strip club and ignored the ice forming in her stomach. "The girls of the Pink Palace were more than happy to oblige." They were, after all, some of her best clients. "Anyway, I should get going or I'll be late."

"Good luck, hon," Thea said, squeezing her on the shoulder.

"You'll knock this one out of the park," Cathy said, pulling her into a hug.

"Thanks, ladies," she said. "I'll see you tomorrow."

She strode out of the locker room, flexing her fingers and rolling her shoulders, trying to get rid of the strange feeling in her gut. It wasn't anything connected to her loan meeting—no, she was fully confident that she would get the money she asked for—but rather, it always came on when she thought about *that* night.

All four of them—her, Stephanie, Thea, and Cathy—were at the strip club to celebrate Stephanie's last few days of freedom. The girls at the club and the manager had been sending their table free drinks, and so maybe she'd indulged herself a little bit. Okay, so maybe it was *a lot*. But she'd always been the responsible one, the mother hen who took care of everyone, so why couldn't she just let her hair down for one night, to celebrate her friend's happiness?

Waking up the next day with a killer hangover and no memory of what happened had been the second worst feeling in the world. The first? Well, that was when she glanced beside her and realized she wasn't alone.

The memory of that morning still made her cringe in shame. There were flashes of what happened the night before, but not enough to piece together the exact events. *At least I was still wearing my clothes*. An STD from a stranger would have taught her never to drink five vodka cranberries on an empty stomach again. *Or something worse*. An unplanned pregnancy was the last thing she needed.

She had quickly slunk out of bed, meaning to leave the motel room undetected, though curiosity had gotten the best of her. Before she headed for the exit, she glanced back at her companion. *Oh, damn*.

The image of that beautiful man would be forever burned in her mind. Strong jaw, aquiline nose. Golden tanned skin. Broad, muscled chest tapering into a tiny waist and the perfect six-pack. The sprinkling of hair over his lower abdomen teasing downward. He had looked so peaceful, like an angel with his eyes closed. She wondered what the color of his eyes were.

An image of light blue-gray eyes popped into her head, making her start.

What the—

She shook her head. No, she didn't see his eyes that morning. No way she could recall them. Yet, for the last three months, she had thought about the mystery man nearly every day. Sometimes she'd even dream of him, or thought she did anyway, when she woke up in a sweat, her body aching and wanting. For what, she didn't know.

Stop thinking about him, Sarah, and get it together. She pushed all thoughts of him aside, even though she knew it would only be temporary.

Marching into the employee garage, she headed for her car and got in. Soon, she was pulling into one of the empty spaces of the National Bank parking lot and heading toward the front door where a familiar figure was already waiting for her.

"You're here," Darcey exclaimed excitedly.

"Of course I am," she greeted her sister.

Looking at the two of them, no one would guess they were sisters. While Sarah was tall and tanned, Darcey was petite, fair-haired and curvy. Their personalities were also the opposite. Where her sister tended to be flighty and sweet, Sarah was grounded and sarcastic. But there was more to being family than blood, after all. The day they met in that awful foster home twelve years ago, Sarah and Darcey decided they were sisters of the heart.

"God, I'm so nervous," Darcey squawked. "What if something goes wrong? Or if they realize I'm a—"

"Calm down, Darce," Sarah soothed, placing a hand on her sister's back, which always worked to relax her. "No one will realize *anything*." She had protected Darcey and their other adopted sibling, Adam, for over a decade now, and she wasn't going to stop anytime soon. "You're a bright, smart woman, and that business plan you put together surely knocked their socks off."

"*We* put together, but you wrote most it," Darcey reminded her. "I typed it up and printed it out."

"Right. We did, *partner*. You're going to be a great store manager, you know."

"Thank you for believing in me, Sarah," she said, her voice quaking.

"C'mon now," she said, patting her on the shoulder. "Let's go and get this loan."

They walked into the branch, heading straight to the offices off to the side. "Sarah Mendez and Darcey Wednesday here to see Mr. Mack," she said to the secretary sitting at the front.

"He's expecting you, but he just stepped out." She nodded to the empty office behind her. "You can wait for him inside."

They walked inside the glass-walled office and sat on the chairs in front of the desk. They had barely settled in before Harry Mack walked in behind them.

"Ladies," he greeted, his white bushy brows drawn together as he rounded his table and sat on his worn leather chair. When they first came here to apply for the business loan, Harry Mack seemed like a kind, affable guy in his mid-fifties. He had been helpful in getting all the paperwork necessary, but there was something about the blank look on his face this morning that set off Sarah's instincts. Darcey must have noticed, too, because of her *perceptive* nature, and she began to fidget.

"Good morning, Mr. Mack." Sarah did her best to sound cheerful and optimistic. "So, I hope you have those loan papers ready, because I'm ready to sign."

He folded his hands over the table and leaned forward. "Ms. Mendez, Ms. Wednesday," he began. "I don't know quite how to say this, so let me get straight to the point so I won't waste your time. Your loan application has been denied."

"No. You can't—" Darcey let out an inhuman cluck and she slapped her hands over her mouth as Mack raised a brow at her.

Sarah reached over and gripped her sister's hand. *Keep it together, Darcey,* she pleaded silently. Despite the dreaded words and the fact that her dream was about to be shattered, Sarah managed to remain calm. "Mr. Mack, I don't understand. When we came here last week to give you the final documents and requirements, you practically said we were a shoo-in. Now you're saying we've been denied. Can you please explain to us what happened between then and now?"

Mack cleared his throat. "Upon further investigation, we realized that there was something you failed to disclose on your application. And as you may or may not know, falsification of loan documents is a crime."

"No," Darcey jumped to her feet. "Please, you can't ..."

Sarah rushed to put herself between her sister and Mack. Gripping her arms, she shook Darcey gently. "Sweetie, calm down." Her stomach turned to lead as she saw the change in her sister's eyes. Red seeped in from the outside like ink, filling up the cornea until it reached her pupils, turning her eyes into bloody wells.

"It's my fault," she cried. "I should have told them. We shouldn't have hidden *what* I am."

Sarah's heart plummeted. "It's not, Darce," she said. "Please ... calm down before you ..."

Mack cleared his throat behind them. "If you need a few minutes ..."

Sarah squared her shoulders. "We're fine." She stared at Darcey. "Sweetie, you're fine. Everything's going to be just fine. Shh ..." She leaned down. "I love you, no matter what. Sisters forever, okay?"

That seemed to work as Darcey went limp. "I'm ... fine," she whispered. "She's fine. She's not going to come out."

"Good." Satisfied, she gently led Darcey back down to her chair, then turned to face Mack. *Damned prejudiced sons of bitches*, she cursed silently. She'd protected Darcey all these years, and she wasn't going to stop now. "Now, you were about to explain, Mr. Mack?"

The loan officer's nostrils flared. "I was. Take a seat—"

"Just say what it is that we 'failed to disclose.'" *Let us know what bigots you guys are.* "Because as far as I know, there wasn't a question on your loan application whether we're human or shifters."

Mack's jaw practically dropped to the ground. "E-excuse me?"

"That's what is it, right?" she accused. "You found out Darcey's a shifter, and you're denying our loan because of that?"

"What?" Mack slammed his palms on the desk in indignation. "Ms. Mendez, we at National Bank do not discriminate against shifters. Why, we don't even ask that in any of our paperwork. The ACLU would have our heads."

"Then why did you deny the application?"

"Because, Ms. Mendez"—he opened the file sitting on top of his desk and flipped it over to her, pointing at the top of the first page—"you wrote here that you were single. But, upon further investigation, we found out that that was simply untrue."

"What? Of course it's true. I think I would remember if I was married," she scoffed.

"When our investigators did a search, your name came up in the civil registry." He rifled through the papers and took out another sheet. "There. See? That's your name and signature, on this marriage certificate dated three months ago."

Her gaze dropped down the paper. *Oh. Fuck.* There it was. *Sarah Mendez of Nevada.* And that was definitely her signature at the bottom. "But there has to be—" *Fuck!* The date on the certificate made her stomach sink. *Oh, no. Oh, no. Oh no.*

"Sarah?" Darcey asked. "Is it true? Did you get married?"

"I ... uh ..." *Satan's balls*, what did she get herself into? "I ...

can explain." *Kind of.* "But why does it matter if I'm married? This is a business loan and I'm not asking my—" she gulped, "husband to co-sign. Surely, lots of people who are married get loans by themselves?"

"Ms. Mendez, Nevada is a community property state. Even if your husband has no plans to co-sign or give you money, or even be involved in your business, you still have to disclose your civil status. Now," he leaned back in his chair. "Seeing as you seem to be ... surprised at this development, and let's be honest, this is Las Vegas," he said with a knowing grin, "I won't recommend pressing charges."

"That's one load off my mind," she said, plopping back on the chair. "But our loan? What's going to happen? Can I just resubmit the paperwork?"

"Not with us, I'm afraid," he said. "But I could recommend another bank. I have a colleague down by First Federal that could help you. You already have copies of the paperwork, that'll give you a head start."

"Thank you." It wasn't what she wanted, but at least all was not lost, except maybe some time.

"You're welcome. But, before you do proceed, seeing as I mentioned Nevada being community property, might I suggest a speedy divorce or annulment so you can get things in order? Uncontested, you can have it done in a matter of days."

"Sounds good," she said. Now the only thing she needed to do was figure out who her husband was. "I'll get on it. Thank you, Mr. Mack. Would you mind if I, uh, borrow this?" He nodded, and she swiped the marriage certificate. "Let's go, Darcey."

Spinning on her heel, she marched out of the office, walking past the tellers and customers, then breezed through the glass doors and headed out into the early morning heat of the desert.

Numbness flowed through her, thankfully, as it kept all the emotions she was holding inside at bay.

"Sarah?" came Darcey's quiet voice. "Are you okay?"

Snapping out of her trance, she jerked back. "Yeah. I mean. I guess? Fuck!" she cursed, crumpling the paper in her hand. "Shit. Goddammit!"

Darcey, bless her heart, placed an arm around her shoulder and hugged her close. "It'll be all right, Sarah," she soothed. "Don't worry, we'll figure it out. But how are you feeling?"

And this was the reason why she loved Darcey more than life itself. She never judged, never berated or belittled anyone. Her heart was big enough to contain the world. "I'm ... I just ..." Tears burned at her throat. She just wanted something to go her way for once, damn it! All she wanted to do was provide a better life for Darcey, Adam, and herself.

Well, Sarah didn't know the meaning of giving up. Ever since she'd been abandoned by her parents at the age of four, she'd been fighting for everything she had, and she was damn well going to keep fighting if that's what it took. "I'll figure this out, Darce. Don't you worry."

"Mr. Mack said he'd help us and that we could just submit the same paperwork," Darcey said. "Which means we're just going to be delayed by a little bit."

"A week at most," Sarah estimated. "Three days if we work our butts off."

"Let's get to work then," Darcey suggested. "I can reprint the business plan at the library and change the cover page. Let me go and ask Mr. Mack for his friend's name at First Federal."

"Good," she said, patting her sister on the arm. "You go ahead and I'll wait here. We'll go to the library and then pick up Adam at school."

Darcey worried her plump lower lip. "What will we tell him?"

"Er, definitely nothing about ... this," she said, waving the crumpled piece of paper. "We'll just say that we got a better offer from another bank."

"Right." Her sister gave her the thumbs-up. "Okay, give me a minute, I'll get that info from Mr. Mack."

As she disappeared back into the bank, Sarah's shoulders sank. *God, what the hell did I do?*

"Apparently, I got married," she said aloud. "Fuck my life." She leaned her forehead against the cool glass windows of the building. Of course, it happened during the night of the bachelorette party. How trashed was she? Very. So wasted, she didn't even remember getting married.

With a sigh, she uncrumpled the paper in her hand, her eyes immediately scanning down to the name next to hers. "Daniel Rogers of Colorado," she said aloud, as if doing so would conjure him up. If only it did, then this would solve her problems. Divorces and annulments were just as easy to obtain as marriages in Nevada. She bet getting married while drunk was probably grounds for either. *This is Vegas,* she thought, repeating Harry Mack's words.

With a determined grunt, she straightened her spine and stared down at the name again. Finally, she had a name to go with the face. *Who are you, Daniel Rogers?* Well, she was about to find out.

They said ending a marriage wasn't easy, but this was getting *ridiculous*.

A week passed since the day at the bank Sarah found out she was married. Being a broke waitress, the first thing she did was turn to the Internet and Google "quickie annulment" and "fast divorce." The paperwork could be done in minutes and the process finished quickly even without the other party's signature—if she had the money for an attorney.

She had no choice but to do it herself which meant wading through the bureaucracy and hoping she could do it all without making any mistakes. Without her "husband's" signature, the process could take four months. But the fastest way to do it would be to actually have the other party sign and file the paperwork for the uncontested annulment and have everything done in a week.

So, she thought she'd try to find Daniel Rogers of Colorado by herself, but that was like digging through a haystack for the proverbial needle. Social media was a bust, so she tried one of those people finder websites. There were about eighty-nine people named Daniel Rogers from Colorado, and without a middle name or birthday, she couldn't narrow it down. Plus she had to pay that website to unlock each name so she could get an address and phone number.

"I guess I should take out that emergency credit card." She winced, thinking about what it would cost to get those numbers. What if the right Daniel Rogers turned out to be number eighty-nine? Or what if he put down a fake name and she never found him at all?

"We'll find a way," Darcey assured her. They were sitting at their favorite diner just off The Strip, commiserating over greasy eggs, home fries, and potatoes."

"Even if we did find a way, what should I say? Hi, Daniel, did you happen to be in Las Vegas about three months ago and have no memory of getting married? Surprise, I'm your wife."

"Cheer up," Darcey said. "We'll fix this. You could still file the annulment without his signature, right?"

"Yeah, but that means spending money we can't afford on attempting to find him to serve the papers and waiting up to four months for the judgement from family court, which is time we don't have."

"I'm sure the owner of the space we want to lease will give us some time until we get the loan if we ask him," Darcey suggested.

Sweet, sweet Darcey. The poor girl could really be naive sometimes, which was why Sarah had to keep looking out for her; lots of people tended to take advantage of her sister. But real estate was at a premium around here, at least good boutique space in a nice area that didn't cost and arm and a leg *and* a spleen.

"Sure, we can try that, but if I can find this guy then all he has to do is sign it, and it'll all be done in a week. The loan papers are already with Mr. Ross at First Federal, and all we have to do is tell him to put them through." Meeting with their new loan officer had been the bright spot in their week.

"Maybe we can dip into our savings, just a little bit. Or I can ask my boss for a loan." Darcey worked at a children's clothing boutique in one of the casino shops.

"I don't want you owing Agnes anything," Sarah replied, distaste in her voice. "You know that hag will lord it over you." If they didn't need the health insurance so badly, she would have told her sister to quit working for that bitch long ago. Agnes was definitely one of those people who abused Darcey's good nature, often asking her to work overtime without pay or extra work a manager shouldn't be doing.

A hopeless feeling came over Sarah, and she slumped back in her seat. God, awful didn't even begin to describe how she felt. *I'm supposed to take care of them.* It was a vow she made long ago. And now, she was letting them down.

"Don't worry, Sarah," Darcey said. "We'll figure it out. How about—"

"Hey, turn up the news!" a shout came from behind.

Sarah frowned as the TV above the counter blasted with the familiar "Breaking News" bumper from the local TV news station. "What the heck is going on?"

Darcey's eyes went wide. "Shh, I wanna hear this."

"Hear what?" Turning around, she focused on the screen as the anchor came on.

"And this just in," the pretty blonde anchor began. *"We now have a confirmed identity on the man who foiled the assassination attempt on Vice President Scott Baker this morning as he was making a speech during a campaign stopover in Blackstone, Colorado."*

"What?" Sarah exclaimed. "Someone tried to kill the Vice President?" After her overnight shift, she'd crashed for a couple of hours at home, then came here to meet Darcey for a late lunch.

"Yeah, it's been all over the news this morning," her sister said. "Look, they're playing the footage again."

A video, obviously taken from a cellphone camera, showed the handsome young VP on a stage delivering a speech from behind a podium. Suddenly, someone from the audience hopped on stage and charged at him with a gun. Before he could reach the VP, a fast-moving brown blur came from out of nowhere, tackling the would-be assassin down to the ground. Screams could be heard from the background as the camera pulled away from the stage, the footage turning into a shaky blend of trees, sky, running people, and then dirt as the phone landed on the ground.

"Holy shit." That was intense.

"The Blackstone Police Department has put out a statement and identified the previously-unknown savior." The anchor's face disappeared as the headshot of a man filled the screen. *"That man's name is—"*

"Daniel Rogers," Sarah said at the same time, her heart slamming into her chest.

"Sarah?" Darcey asked, her delicate blonde brows snapping together.

Everything around her seemed to stop as a buzzing sound filled her ears. For a second, she thought she was imagining things, but no. That face ... there was no mistaking it. That was definitely the man she woke up next to in that motel three months ago.

Her husband.

"It's him," she whispered, unable to break her gaze from the screen. Though the image had been replaced with a commercial break, it was still burned into her mind. And those eyes—silvery blue, just as she thought she'd remembered. And then more memories came slamming back into her brain at the same time.

Strong arms wrapping around her.

Firm lips on hers.

The cotton fabric of a shirt, warm from the heat of golden tanned skin.

You. Only you from now on.

"Sarah!"

Fingers snapping in front of her face jerked her out of the memory. "Oh God."

"The anchor said his name was ... was that him?" Darcey asked, her blue eyes widening. "Your hus—"

"Yes," she confirmed, slumping back in her seat. "Oh God." Her nerve endings felt frazzled, and hot and cold flushes alternated in her system. Somehow, when he was just a faded memory and a name, it was like he was a figment of her imagination. But now, it all came crashing down. The reality of it all, the consequences of her one night of indiscretion. "Fuck my life."

"This is great!" Darcey clapped her hands together.

"Great? What do you mean, great? This whole thing is a disaster."

"No, no." Darcey shook her head, her light blonde curls bouncing against her soft cheeks. "I mean, now you know who he is. Just wait a few minutes and Google his name again. All those news sites will have all his details, and you'll be able to find him. Then you can go and ask him to sign the papers, and *voilà*, instant annulment."

A strange thrill of excitement coursed through her veins at the thought of going to him. *What the hell?* Excitement? What was she thinking?

"Well?" Darcey asked. "Are you going to do it? Seems like it's the best solution to our problems."

And that was how Sarah found herself, days later, driving out to Blackstone Colorado.

Just as Darcey had predicted, information about Daniel Rogers was splashed all over the Internet the next couple of hours after he was identified. While she thought he was a cop or Secret Service Agent, turns out he was some kind of forest ranger. Pictures of him looking dashing in his khaki uniform were everywhere—from social media sites to local news reports, and she tried her best to ignore that stab of desire in her gut, then told herself it was a blessing, not a disappointment, that she didn't sleep with him that night. Not that she would have remembered anyway.

After getting all the necessary papers ready, she set off for Colorado. She left before dawn and arrived eleven hours later. Exhausted from driving nearly non-stop for half a day, she drove into the small Main Street area of the town.

Blackstone seemed like a lovely place, with its cute little houses and gorgeous mountain scenery now lush and green in the full bloom of summer. But there was no time to be idle and explore; she planned to find Daniel Rogers, have him sign the annulment papers she had in her purse, and then drive back in the morning after getting a couple hours' sleep at the motel she had booked online.

As she drove down searching for a place to grab a quick bite to eat and figure out how to find her soon-to-be ex, she saw a place called Rosie's Bakery and Cafe. It sounded like a good place to stop, so she parked in the lot behind the building, and walked inside.

Wow. It was only four o'clock, and the place was already busy. The waitress in front informed her it was half an hour's wait to get a table, but she was so tired, she didn't want to go anywhere else, so she sat in the waiting area, drinking sips of the free water they offered. Finally, her name was called, and she got up.

"Sarah, party of one?" the pretty older woman in a retro-style dress asked. The name tag on her chest proclaimed her name as Rosie, which meant she was probably the owner herself. "Sorry for the wait, but it's high season, and we've been getting a record number of visitors."

"No worries," she said. "I'm famished. Just need something to eat and some coffee."

"You've come to the right place," she said as she led Sarah to a spacious booth. "Now, we specialize in pies here"—she nodded to the glass display counter that was filled with pies —"so I can have one to you in a jiffy. We have the usual—apple, pecan, sweet potato, peach, blueberry, lemon meringue, chicken or beef pot pie. Our specials for the day are cherry lemon, dragonfruit, and Bear-y Hero pie."

"Berry pie?" she asked.

"*Bear*-y Hero pie," she chuckled. "Like the animal. It's named for a local celebrity. But yeah, it has blueberries, strawberries, and boysenberries."

"Um, I'll just have a slice of the apple pie and coffee,

please," she said.

"Coming right up, sugar."

Sarah waited a few minutes, then Rosie came back with her order, which she finished in minutes. Not wanting to waste any more time, she turned her head, searching for Rosie so she could ask for the check. However, something—or rather, someone—caught her eye in the booth behind her. The blond man facing her was wearing a familiar khaki uniform, as was his companion.

Rangers. Like Daniel Rogers. Were they coworkers? On impulse, she cleared her throat. "Excuse me. Are you guys rangers?" Her gaze dropped knowingly to their uniforms.

It was the other guy—the dark haired one right behind her—who spoke. "This guy"—he jerked his thumb at his friend —"isn't anymore, but I am." He wiggled a brow at her. "What can I do for you, sweetheart?"

Oh, brother. She recognized that gleam of interest in the man's eyes, having seen it many times from players at the casinos. However, she also knew how to use that to her advantage. Smoothing down her lacy top, she slid out of the booth and turned to face them. "I was wondering," she said sweetly, "do you guys know where I can find Daniel Rogers?"

The dark-haired man's face fell and he slumped back. "I'm so *fucking* tired of hearing that name."

The blond man rolled his eyes. "Sorry about my friend, he's a drama king. Can I ask why you need to know where he is?"

She detected no hint of attraction from Blondie, so she switched tactics. Crossing her arms under her chest, she gave him a challenging stare. "You could."

Seconds ticked by as they played a silent game of chicken. When Blondie shrugged, she knew she'd won. "He should be at HQ—that's the Blackstone Rangers Headquarters," he said. "It's on the road that leads up to the mountains, you can't miss it."

Finally. "Thank you." Pivoting on her heel, she dropped a

couple of bills on the table and then headed toward the exit. However, a voice calling out to her made her stop.

"Hey, baby, what do you need him for when I'm here?" It was the dark-haired ranger. "Those tats are a piece of art, you know." He nodded at her arm. "And so are you. Maybe I can—"

"Nail me to the wall?" she finished with a scoff. "Please. Like I haven't heard that one before." Sadly, she wished she was joking, but it was one of the hazards of her job. However, soon she would have her own business and shop, and she would no longer have to endure catcalls, innuendoes, pinches, and gropes from horny gamblers. But first, she needed to find Daniel Rogers so he could sign the annulment papers.

Heading back to her car, she was about to reach for the door handle when she heard someone running up behind her.

"Miss! Hey, miss!"

Turning, she let out an exasperated grunt when she saw who it was. "If it wasn't obvious, let me make it plainer: I'm not interested." she said to the dark-haired Ranger. He was attractive, she had to give him that, but she had other things to do right now.

The man skidded to a halt in front of her. "Whoa!" He held his hands up defensively. "I wasn't going to hit on you again."

"Then why are you following me?"

"I want to help you," he said. "Find Rogers, I mean."

She eyed him suspiciously. "Why?"

"Why would I help you?" he asked. "Why not? But why are you looking for him?"

"I'm just ..." She bristled. "I just need to speak with him. That's all. I'm not going to hurt him or anything."

His eyes narrowed. "Talk to him, huh? Well, you won't be able to get near him or past the door, but I can get you in, no prob. But, you're not a crazy stalker or a reporter trying to catch him doing something bad, are you?"

"I don't have any bad intentions, I swear. I just need a few minutes of his time."

There was something about the way he looked at her that was unnerving. Like he was sizing her up. She wondered if there was more to this guy than meets the eye. "All right, just follow me," he nodded at the dark blue pickup truck parked a few spaces away, "And I'll lead you up to HQ and get you inside so you can talk to Daniel."

"I ... thank you, uh ..."

"Anders," he said, holding out a hand. "Anders Stevens. And you are?"

She hesitated, but shook his hand quickly. "Sarah."

"Sarah ...?"

"Just Sarah," she said.

"All right, sweetheart," he began. "It's about a forty-five-minute drive. Try to keep up." Pivoting on his heel, he strode off toward his truck.

Sarah bit her lip, hoping she wasn't making a mistake. Still, the thought of facing Daniel Rogers was making her stomach tie up in knots. Truthfully, she didn't know what she was going to say to him. Did he remember her at all? Or would he believe her? Well, she had the marriage certificate, and surely, he would at least remember being in Vegas that weekend. All he needed to do was sign the papers, and they would never have to see each other again.

With a deep, calming breath, she got into her car and turned the key in the ignition to start the engine. Still, it did nothing to soothe her nerves or make the butterflies in her stomach disappear. *Just think of the loan, the business, the boutique,* she told herself. *Think of Darcey not having to work for Agnes anymore. Think of being able to afford insurance and doctor visits for Adam.* For them, she would do anything.

Chapter 3

Daniel let out an unhappy grunt as he shuffled the papers around on the desk for what seemed like the hundredth time that afternoon. Feeling fed up, he pushed them away and propped his chin on his hands. *God, I hate desk duty.* But he didn't exactly have a choice. Well, it was this or take a couple of days off, but he knew they were already short-handed as it was with the influx of visitors to the mountains. Which of course, was his fault.

He groaned and buried his face in his palms. *All I wanted to do was stop an assassin, not turn my life into a circus. What was I thinking?*

Actually, he wasn't thinking in that particular moment. When he saw someone jump on the stage with a gun, pure instinct had driven him to stop the man before he could do any harm. Really, he knew anyone would have done it, and he just happened to be at the right place, at the right time.

With the vice president's visit, security was tight around town and the Blackstone Police Department had asked the rangers for volunteers to help with crowd control. He had signed up because it sounded like a cool opportunity. They assigned him right up front near the stage. VP Baker had been in the middle of the speech when the man in the hoodie jumped up on stage.

Daniel had seen the glint of the gun in his hand and leapt up on the stage and tackled him. Secret service agents swarmed them in seconds, and then everything erupted into chaos. He'd been taken into custody, mostly for his own safety, and after a few hours of being interviewed by the head of the VP's secret service detail, they released him. And when he got out, his life had turned completely upside down.

First, it was the reporters. They ambushed him as he left the precinct and shoved cameras and microphones in his face. Then they followed him as he went home, and he rushed inside without talking to them. It was only when he turned on the TV and checked his phone, he realized the how bad it was. The video of him tackling the assassin and his picture from the official Blackstone Ranger website were all over the news and Internet.

He thought it would all die down by morning, but it got worse. Apparently, he had become some sort of celebrity, and aside from the reporters camping outside his home and the Blackstone HQ, they were also inundating his phone and the lines at work, trying to get him to do interviews or TV appearances.

The media was easy to ignore, but the ordinary people coming up to him while he was trying to shop or go out to eat or just do his errands were the worst. He couldn't even get gas without being stopped and asked for a selfie or a chat. Raised to be polite, he couldn't tell them to buzz off even though he was getting tired of it all.

Now they were bothering him at work too. Though Blackstone Mountain was private property, it was open to visitors who wanted to go camping, explore the forests and trails or hike up to Contessa Peak. Summers were always busy, but now they were seeing an influx of visitors who all wanted to get a glimpse of the man who saved the vice president. When some overeager admirers rushed into the offices when they saw Daniel, Damon Cooper, the chief of the Blackstone Rangers, declared he'd had enough and put him on desk duty, away from the public eye.

His grizzly was not happy being cooped inside.

Yeah, well neither am I.

Actually, his bear had been acting strange the past couple of months. He'd never really had a problem with his inner grizzly; his father had taught him all the basics of controlling the bear but not smothering it, allowing it to have freedom, but not enough to take over. In fact, he'd always gotten along with his animal, and they worked as a team, making him really good at his job.

But lately, the grizzly inside him had been moody, irritable, and downright unpleasant sometimes. The smallest things would set if off, and he was having a hard time keeping it in check.

And frankly, if he was honest, he felt strange too. Perhaps it was those weird dreams he'd been having.

It was hard to describe them really. It was all flashes of something. Black lace. Warm tawny skin inked with a yellow, blue, and red design. Gloriously thick caramel hair. Plump lips. Or a feeling or a sweet scent he couldn't name. He'd wake up sweating and aroused, but at the same time, like there was a hole in his chest that he couldn't fill. Maybe it had been too long since he'd been with a woman. He had a few numbers on his phone he could easily call, girls who were always up for a night of fun, but he couldn't bring himself to contact any of them. In fact, his inner bear practically tore him up from the inside if he even thought of finding relief with anyone.

Drumming his fingers on the table, he shoved the chair back and got to his feet. Being in here bored him to death, but he couldn't go out and do his real job. *May as well get outta here and get some work done around the house.*

Two years ago, when his parents had retired to Texas, they left him their sprawling five-bedroom house, and he had begun renovating and updating it himself in his free time. It was almost ready, and he only needed to work on the backyard and decorating the interior, but he couldn't bring himself to give up his apartment and move in. Sure, it had been his childhood home, but he knew his parents had left it to him with the intention of one day filling it with his own family. "Don't let us wait too long to hold our grandkids, now, you hear?" Dad had told him with a wink.

Did he want children? Sure he did, but he was still enjoying his career and was hoping to get a promotion as Damon's deputy. Plus, he was hoping to find his mate like his parents had found each other, but it felt like he'd been searching forever and that he'd never find her.

His grizzly protested at that. *Hmmm*, he never knew his animal was an optimist.

Putting those thoughts aside, he sent Damon a quick email telling him he was punching out early and headed toward the locker room. After a quick shower, he wrapped a towel around his waist and went to his locker to change into street clothes.

It wasn't near shift change, so the locker room was empty. However, he was about to take off his towel when he heard the door open.

"... his truck's still in the lot and the office is empty, so he's probably in here," someone said. He recognized the speaker as Anders Stevens.

" ... I'm sure—wait, isn't this a locker room?"

The second speaker was a woman, and as soon as he heard

her voice, his entire spine went rigid and the hairs on his entire body stood up. Why did that voice sound familiar?

"Yeah it is," Anders replied. "So what?"

"I mean, is this the men's locker?"

"Well, Rogers isn't going to be in the women's locker, that much I can tell you."

What the hell was going on? Slamming his locker shut, he turned toward the sound of the voices. "What the hell do you—"

Mine.

"—want?" Every nerve ending in his body frazzled as various synapses in his brain fired up. His grizzly roared and stood up on its hind legs, paws raised in victory.

It was her.

His mate.

She'd walked in here like he'd summoned her from out of thin air. But why did this feel like *déjà vu*? Like it had happened before and he'd stared into her chocolate brown eyes before, seen her pretty face and plump lips. Like he already knew what that smooth tawny skin felt like and how her curvy body fit against his.

She looked stunned too. Human, he could tell, which meant she didn't hear the call of an animal declaring them as mates. Her gaze dropped down to the towel around his waist, and she quickly jerked her head up, but not before he saw her pink tongue flick out to lick her lips.

Fffffuuuck. He turned around, opened his locker and grabbed for his jeans, placing them over the front of his hips before he embarrassed himself. "Uh, can I help you?" *Mate. She's our mate!* He still couldn't believe it.

"Yes, you can, actually," she replied. Her voice was low and smoky, and it sent pleasant tingles across his skin. "I need to talk to you."

"Sure," he said. "Anders, do you mind?"

The other ranger crossed his arms over his chest. "No, I don't actually," he said, flashing him a grin. "Go ahead."

"Anders," he warned. What was the tiger shifter doing here anyway? With his *mate*? His inner bear did not like that and bared its teeth at Anders. "Privacy, please."

When Daniel didn't budge, Anders shrugged. "Fine. See you later, sweetheart," he said to the woman before he turned and left.

Daniel reined in his grizzly before it could take a swipe at Anders. *Calm down. Our mate is here!* Speaking of which ... "So." He cleared his throat. "What can I do for you?" *Aside from keeping you and moving you into my den?*

"It's you," she said, almost reverently. "It's really you."

"Me?" Did she recognize him as her mate?

"Yes. Um, maybe you don't remember. My name is Sarah. Three months ago, you were in Vegas, and we ... we met at The Pink Palace."

Realization swept through him. The memories slammed back into him all at the same time. Her skin. Those lips. Even the sleeve tattoo on her arm—that of a woman wearing red and blue surrounded by a halo of yellow—lit up something in his brain telling him he'd seen her before.

And those eyes. Those eyes that had been haunting his dreams.

"Yes," he gasped. God, this was it. The moment he'd been waiting for. But why couldn't he remember—oh right. The drugs.

When he arrived back from Vegas, the first thing he did was go to the hospital in Blackstone and get a drug test. They confirmed that he had trace amounts of bloodsbane in his system. He was almost certain that it was that asshole from the club who slipped it in his drink, to get back at him for spoiling his plans with the stripper.

He called The Pink Palace and told them what happened. To his surprise, the management took him seriously. They found the CCTV footage of that punk going outside and collecting something from a car that drove by, then going back in and putting it in a drink. They were also able to identify him and banned him for life, plus pressed charges on Daniel's behalf, even using their own lawyer to represent him.

But then, he didn't realize it could make him forget everything—including meeting his mate.

"So, you're probably wondering why I'm here," she began, twirling a lock of caramel hair between her fingers.

"Er, yeah." Though he wasn't going to complain. Maybe she did feel the pull of the mating? And she obviously recognized him. Shit, he didn't even remember her face until now.

"I saw you on the news and—and ... this is embarrassing," she said. "So, we met at The Pink Palace Gentlemen's Club in Vegas. My friends and I were celebrating because one of us was getting married. And I was pretty wasted, and I think you were too."

"Uh, kinda," he said.

"Anyway, I can't remember anything from that night. Do you?"

"Er, not much," he said. "I woke up in a motel room, alone."

Her cheeks turned pink. "Yeah, I'm sorry. I mean, I figured you might not want to wake up to me and my mascara raccoon eyes." She gave a nervous chuckle. "So, I slipped out before you woke up. But, I'm here because something happened that night."

"Yes?" Did it? He remembered having his pants on, and there was no indication they'd had sex. *Shit!* Maybe they did earlier, before they wound up at that motel room.

"And I've been looking for you to let you know. I didn't

know where to begin, then you showed up on TV, and I realized who you were."

"Okay, and now you—" *Oh God.* They had a one-night stand neither could remember and now she was looking for him. His gaze dropped down to her belly. *She was pregnant. With his cub.*

"So, I was—hey, what are you looking at?" She sucked in a deep breath and covered her abdomen with her arms. "I am *not* pregnant, you jerk. We didn't even have sex!"

"We didn't?" he asked, disappointment pouring through him.

"No, we didn't," she huffed. "I would remember that part at least. And I was wearing my clothes, and you had on most of yours when I woke up."

"Oh." Was she really here then because they were mates?

Her hands dropped to her sides. "I can't explain it ... I'm so embarrassed."

Hope filled his chest. "It's all right," he said soothingly. "You can tell me." *I understand.* At least, now he could. That emptiness inside him for months. That longing feeling for something he didn't know. Now he knew. He'd been missing his mate since they parted. And now here they were, together again.

"I can't say ..." She buried her face in her hands. "I don't know why I can't just say it."

"Just say it, baby doll." He resisted the urge to reach out and touch her. There would be time enough for that. "You can say it." *You're my mate. You need me as much as I need you.*

With a long sigh, she lowered her hands. "I need you ..."

Yes! "Need me to what?"

"I need you so badly to—"

Mate you. Bond you. Be with you and only you from now on.

"Sign these papers."

"I do too," he sighed. "Wait, *what*?" He blinked as she dug into her purse and pulled out an envelope. "Papers?"

"Yeah, they're annulment papers."

"Annulment of what?"

Her nostrils flared as her cheeks flushed. "Of our marriage."

"Excuse me?"

"Our marriage."

He heard her the first time, of course, but the information wasn't connecting in his brain. "We're *married*?"

"Check out the last page." She waved the envelope at him, and he snatched it from her hands. "That's our ... marriage certificate."

Flipping through the other pages, he reached the last page and began to read aloud. "The Original Chapel of Hearts Las Vegas ... this is to certify ... Daniel Rogers of Colorado ... Sarah Mendez of Nevada ... lawful—"

"Wedlock," she finished as she bit her lip. "That's a certified copy by the way. And I checked with that chapel myself. They, uh, said they were waiting for us to come back and pick up the rings we had engraved. But anyway, I'm sure you want to be married as much as I do, so let's just sign these papers and the judge will grant the annulment in a week."

Married. He had gotten married to his mate. And now she wanted an annulment.

His grizzly did *not* like that. It growled and raked its claws down his insides in protest. *Fuck!* Well, he didn't like it either, but it was obvious they had both been too intoxicated to consent to the marriage, and that just felt *wrong*. Pops would be terribly disappointed to hear he'd taken advantage of a woman that way.

But still, it would mean that once their marriage was annulled, she would walk away from him forever, and he couldn't have *that*.

"Er, listen, can we talk about this?"

Her arms folded under her chest. "What is there to talk about? I have a pen right here, and you can sign it, then I can be on my way."

No! Every instinct in his body protested.

"What do you mean *no*?" Her eyes narrowed at him.

Crap, he said that out loud. "I mean ..." *Shit, shit, shit. Think Rogers!* "We can't talk about it right now. I—" In an act of pure desperation, he dropped his jeans and the towel around his waist to the ground.

Her eyes went wide as they briefly lowered. "What the—" She covered her eyes with her hand and spun around. "What the hell are you doing?"

He couldn't stop the smile on his face at her reaction. There was *definitely* interest there. "Oops. Slipped. That's what happens in men's locker rooms, you know."

"Put some clothes on," she ordered. "Now."

"I will, but listen, baby doll, why don't you wait for me outside?" he suggested. "I just need to get dressed. Unless you wanna keep talking here."

Her spine tensed, and her fingers curled into a fist at her side. "I—fine."

As she marched off, he couldn't help watching her generous hips sway gently, making his cock twitch painfully. When the door closed behind her, he let out a groan and knocked his forehead on the locker next to his.

Signing those papers was the right thing to do. He'd been drugged, and she was drunk; neither of them had been in the right mind to consent. But the idea of his mate walking away from him forever didn't seem right at all. The human, logical part of him said he could always try to win her later on, but she lived all the way in Las Vegas, and his life was here in Blackstone. He couldn't imagine leaving everything here behind, but at the same time, Sarah was his mate.

Straightening his posture, he began to dress in his everyday clothes. Maybe he could talk her into having dinner and tell her about the mate stuff. *Explain it to her, see how she reacts and consider her feelings on the matter*. It was the right thing to do. If she didn't want him—a thought that made his stomach clench—then he would have to respect that and move on. It wasn't like he wouldn't be able to find someone else, someone who would love him and he could love back, have children with and grow old with.

Try as he might, however, he couldn't picture it in his head. When he did, the only face that popped into his brain was that of the woman who wanted an annulment from him.

His grizzly snorted smugly.

"I can't," he said aloud to no one in particular. Sarah was her own woman, and she deserved respect. He finished getting ready, slammed his locker shut and walked outside, determined to right this wrong and sign those papers.

That was the plan, anyway, but when he stepped out of the locker room and Sarah turned to face him, his resolve disappeared, only to be replaced by the desire to make this woman truly *his*.

That damned animal inside him chortled tauntingly as if saying *I told you so*.

"Are you done?" she asked, her tone irritated.

One hand planted on her cocked hip, he couldn't help but trace the curves of her body with his gaze, his mind crying out how unfair it was that she could disarm him so just by standing there.

"Um, yeah." He rubbed the back of his head. "Listen, I just got off a long shift." His throat went dry at the lie, but then he reminded himself that *long* was a relative term. "I'm famished. How about we go for a meal somewhere first?"

"You're hungry at a time like this? It'll take two seconds for you to sign." She waved the papers in his face. "I've been driving almost twelve hours, and all I wanna do is crash in my crappy motel room so I can drive back in the morning. I'm already missing a day of work."

He pushed the feelings of guilt aside and pressed on. "So what's another hour or two then? You're probably staying somewhere in town and you have to drive back down anyway. We can stop on Main Street or the nearest restaurant to your motel and sit down and have a chat."

Her plump lips pulled back into a thin line. "Chat? What do we have to chat about?"

God, she was feisty. And he found he liked it. His mate wasn't a pushover. "You don't expect me to sign those papers without reading them, do you? And take the word of a stranger that they're what she says they are? Would you just sign a contract without reading it?"

"Apparently we both did," she snapped back, but then her shoulders sank. "I'm sorry. I'm just stressed out."

The vulnerability that passed over her face made his heart ache. She looked like she bore the weight of the world on her shoulders. He longed to reach out and comfort her, but clenched and unclenched his fingers instead. "I'm sorry for making this difficult. But I just need a couple minutes to sit down and read the papers. I should make my own copies, right? Why don't I take pictures and send them to my dad so he could look it over?"

"Your dad?"

"Yeah, he's a lawyer," he said. "Retired now, but he'll at least give me some advice. I'll call him on the drive over."

"I guess that's okay," she said. "I'm staying at the Blackstone Pines Motel."

"There's a place called Full Moon Diner not far from there. If we take Seventy-Five from the turnoff, we'll pass right by it.

C'mon, the least I can do is buy you a meal after you drove all the way here."

There was hesitation in her face before she nodded. "All right." She handed him the envelope. "Send it to your father so he can read it while we're driving. My car's in the parking lot outside."

"Okay, let's go." Instinctively, he put a hand on her lower back to lead her toward the exit. Though she froze for a second, she didn't shrug it off and allowed him to walk her toward the double doors. "We should—"

A bright flash blinded him, sending his instincts off. His grizzly didn't like that, and it let its displeasure known with a deep roar rattling from its chest. Meanwhile, he tucked Sarah closer to him, his hand moving up to her shoulder.

"Daniel!" someone called. Various phones, recorders, and cameras were shoved in his face. "Daniel, are you going to put out a statement about how you saved Vice President Baker?"

"What's going on?" Sarah asked as she steadied herself against him.

"Sorry, baby doll," he said through gritted teeth. "I swear these sharks won't leave me alone."

"Daniel, is it true they're inviting you to the White House?"

"Are you getting a medal, Daniel?"

"What can you say about the rumors that the assassination—"

"Daniel, who's this lady with you?"

His protective instinct flared. "Guys, can you leave us alone, please? I told you, no comment."

"She's hot," one of the male reporters said with a gleam in his eyes that Daniel did not care for. "Sister? Cousin?"

"Kissing cousins?" someone offered that made the crowd laugh.

"Miss, what's your name?" The male reporter asked,

inching closer to Sarah. "And what's your relationship with America's newest hero?"

"I—"

When Sarah didn't continue her answer and snapped her mouth shut, the reporter shoved his camera closer to her face. "C'mon, sweetheart, give us a pretty smile and tell us—"

Daniel's anger flared when he sensed Sarah's discomfort. "Stay away from my *wife*!" he roared, pushing the nosy reporter away as pure possessive fury filled him.

Silence filled the air for a few seconds, but it took Daniel less time than that to realize he'd screwed up.

"What the hell?" Sarah hissed. "Why did you—"

"Wife?" another reported said. "You're married?"

"That didn't come up in my research."

"When was the wedding?"

"Uh ..." Daniel's brain scrambled. "I—"

"What the hell is going on here?" a booming voice behind them shouted. "May I remind you this is private property? The Blackstone Rangers is not a government agency, and the mountains are private property. Leave Daniel alone, or I'll call the cops."

Relief poured through him as he turned and saw Damon standing in the doorway, arms crossed over his chest, and a menacing look on his face.

"Get us out of here," Sarah ordered. "Now!"

After a quick, grateful nod to Damon, he gripped her shoulders tighter, bowed his head, and swam his way through the crowd around them, shoving people away as he led her to his truck.

"My car's over there," she said.

"Do you want them to know what car you drive and your plate number?" he asked. "Because they won't leave you alone once they find out your name."

"And whose fault is that?" she shot back.

"Look, I'll drive around, and we can find somewhere to lay low for a bit. Damon'll have them dispersed, and we can circle back to get your car."

"I—fine."

He opened the passenger side door for her, but she waved his hand away when he attempted to help her in.

"I can get in by myself." Flipping her long, sleek ponytail back, she climbed in.

After the door shut, he walked around slowly, trying to figure out what to do now. He hadn't meant to blurt out she was his wife, but seeing another male so close to her drove him and his grizzly crazy.

And now, he'd ruined things. How was he going to fix this mess?

Or, maybe, you don't have to, a voice inside him seemed to say.

Most people thought Daniel was a "nice guy" and could never do wrong. Indeed, he took pride in that he had principles and took honesty and integrity seriously. *A man wasn't a man without his word and his honor*, Pops used to say.

But sometimes, he thought about what it would be like to be selfish and think of himself first for once. If he just said *fuck it*, and took whatever he wanted.

And he wanted Sarah.

Maybe, just this time, he didn't have to be the good guy. He could bend some of the rules, be more flexible with his principles knowing the outcome would favor him. He could keep Sarah, and all he had to do was stretch the truth a little bit.

Chapter 4

Sarah fumed as she sat inside Daniel's truck, waiting for him to walk around and get into the driver's side. The damned man took his time, slowly trudging around to make his way to the other side.

Man? Well that was one thing to call him, she guessed. When he let out that inhuman roar, she knew he was one of them. *A shifter.* It was obvious now, like a strange feeling that she always knew. Perhaps it was because she grew up with Darcey that she could tell. She knew of a couple regulars at The Griffin who were shifters, plus it was rumored that the owner of the casino himself was one of them, though no one really knew who or what he was. But the idea that Daniel was a shifter never even entered her mind.

Why hadn't they reported that on the news websites she'd read? To be fair, she didn't spend a lot of time reading those articles. She just looked up where Blackstone was and started planning her trip and getting the annulment papers ready, hoping to get this over with as soon as possible.

But, if she were honest with herself, she'd avoided reading the news articles because she didn't want to keep staring at his picture. It seemed the longer she stared into that handsome, movie star face and silvery blue eyes, more bits and pieces from that night came back to her mind.

Do you think maybe we should get out of here? Have some fun of our own? a voice that sounded like her own said.

I'll follow you to the end of the world if you ask me to, baby doll

"Are you all right, Sarah?"

Daniel's voice—his real one—broke into her thoughts. "Yeah, I'm fine." Leaning back into the leather seat, she stared out the window as the engine roared to life, and the truck zipped out of the parking lot. "Hey, where are we going?" They turned into the road in the opposite direction from where she had come from.

He looked up at his rearview mirror. "Somewhere those reporters won't be able to follow."

They drove up the road, going further into the mountains. Sure enough, a couple of news vans were on their tail. Daniel turned off onto a side road, and at the end was an imposing gate that said "Keep Out, Mining Operations in Progress." A man in a khaki ranger uniform popped his head out from the booth on the side, waved to Daniel, and then disappeared. Moments later, the gate swung open, and they drove through. They closed again when they passed.

"That should hold them," Daniel said with a relieved sigh.

"But we can't stay in here forever," she said. "And where is here, anyway?" Oh God, she was deep in the mountains with a stranger, and no one knew where she was. What if Daniel turned out to be some kind of homicidal maniac? Was that why he didn't want to sign the papers right away? She glanced at him, watching his profile. Surely no one that hot could be a serial killer, right?

"We're still in the Blackstone Mountains, but Lennox Corp.

has this area closed off because they mine the blackstone in this area." He turned down off another path. "But us rangers can come in as needed, and I go to this one place sometimes to think." He drove them further down a road, then a few feet later, they emerged from the dense forest and into a clearing.

"Wow," she gasped. They were right near the end of a cliff, where they had a spectacular view of the blue summer sky. "We're so close to the edge."

"Don't worry," he said, turning to her, his silver-blue eyes twinkling. "I would never let you fall."

Her stomach did a flip-flop at his words. *Don't get distracted.* She came here for one reason only. "Why did you tell them I was your wife?"

"Uh, I just ..." He rubbed the back of his head. "It just came out, okay? That guy was getting too close to you—us, and I just wanted him to back off before I did something I would regret."

"You mean like shift into your animal."

That seemed to catch him by surprise. "Y-yeah. How did you know?"

"I ... read about it," she said. "And then I heard you growl."

"Oh. You're not afraid of me, are you?" He sounded almost scared himself. "I would never hurt you. Nor would my grizzly."

So that's what he was. A grizzly bear. The thought of it should have scared her, but it didn't. Though she had no experience with shifters except for Darcey and she was nowhere even near to what a bear was, somehow, she knew he was telling the truth. "I'm not afraid," she said. "But about the annulment papers."

"Yeah, about those. Listen," he began. "The cat's going to be pretty much out of the bag once those guys find out who you are. Believe me, it only took them a couple hours to get my info. But maybe we could help each other out?"

"Help each other out? What do you mean?"

"Yeah, see ... this is embarrassing, but you know, I didn't jump up on that stage intending to become some kind of celebrity. I was just trying to stop someone from getting hurt. But now my world's turned upside down, and I keep getting, uh, propositions."

"Propositions?"

"Yeah. From women. Lots of them. All of them wanting to date, marry, or f—I mean, go to bed with me."

And unfamiliar feeling curled tight in her chest, going all hot and then cold all of a sudden. Just the thought of other women being near him was making her gut twist. "And so what do you want me to do about it?"

"Can't you just ... hold off on the annulment for now and pretend to be my wife? Just for a couple of days until this all blows over?"

"Excuse me?" She stared at him, silent, waiting for the punchline. "Wait, you're serious?"

"Yeah," he said. "I mean, just let them take a few pictures of us going to dinner, buying furniture together. You know, stuff married couples do. Then, when people see it, they'll stop bothering me,"

He was crazy. "If you think a ring on your finger will stop some crazy bitch determined to fu—bed you, then you're too pure for this world, Rogers," she said. "Besides, it's better if we get this over with now, then they can leave you alone."

"Can't you see; they won't leave me alone? I mean, it'll get even worse if it comes out that we got married while drunk in Vegas." He sighed. "I could lose my job."

That pulled a string in her heart, but she couldn't let that affect her. *Think of Darcey and Adam.* They were counting on her. "I'm sorry, Daniel," she said, hardening her heart. "I need to get this annulment done with as soon as possible."

"Is there someone else?"

The tension in the tiny cab of the truck rose up tenfold. She wanted to lie to him, tell him that she had a boyfriend or was engaged to someone. But she couldn't bring herself to say it out loud. "Does it matter? You don't know me, I don't know you, we can't stay married. Don't make me have to go through the ropes and spend money I don't have getting you served. Please." She closed her eyes and thought of her brother and sister. "Just sign the papers, okay?"

Daniel was looking straight out, his hands on the wheel in a death grip. "Fine," he said, his lips thinning. "I'll have my dad look it over tonight, sign it if he says it looks good, and drop it at your motel in the morning."

"Thank you." She breathed a sigh of relief. At least, she thought it was relief. But why was that knot forming in her stomach getting tighter. "Do you think it's safe to go back?"

"Let me check." He reached for the radio receiver on his car. "Charlie, this is Grizzly One. Did anyone try to follow us up past the gates, over?"

"They tried, Grizzly One," came the voice after the crackling sound. "But I turned them away. Over."

"Awesome. Thanks, Charlie. Over. Base, is it all clear? No more reporters?"

"Affirmative, Grizzly One," came another voice, this time it sounded like a female. "You're all clear. Chief kicked out the rest of them. Over."

"Thanks, Base. Over and out." He replaced the receiver and then put the truck in reverse, turning the wheel until they faced the road back into the forest. The rest of the ride was silent, but she didn't really know what else to say.

As soon as they pulled up to her car, she unbuckled her belt. "Thanks," she mumbled.

"Sarah, I—"

"Yes?" she said a little too quickly, whipping her head back at him.

Those silvery blue eyes stared back at her, his lips twitching as if he wanted to say something. "I ... nothing."

Disappointment—over what, she wasn't sure—poured over her like a bucket of ice water. Afraid to say something else, she nodded, and quickly hopped out and made a dash for her own car.

Safe inside, she started the engine. Daniel hadn't moved from his spot, and though she couldn't see him, it was as if she could feel his silvery blue gaze on her.

It's done, she told herself as she pulled out of the spot. By this time tomorrow, she'd be home, annulment papers in hand. She'd be free of this farce and move on with her life, without Daniel Rogers in it.

Sarah spent much of the evening tossing and turning, unable to quiet her thoughts. Of course, she was thinking of Daniel and that inscrutable look on his face when he told her he'd sign the papers.

Why did he seem almost disappointed? Did he not want to get this whole thing over with? And what was with the crazy plan of his to use her as some kind of shield from all those women throwing themselves at him?

The thought of anyone propositioning him was enough to put her in a bad mood. *He should just sleep with them.* It sounded like any guy's dream, having hordes of attractive girls lining up for a chance to fuck him. Yet it made something inside her want to explode in fury.

She must have exhausted herself at some point because eventually she fell asleep. The sound of her phone ringing woke her up, and it took her a second to remember where she was. *Blackstone. Motel. Daniel Rogers.*

Pushing him from her thoughts, she reached for the phone on the bedside table. "Hello?" she greeted groggily.

"Sarah, where are you?" came Darcey's frantic cry through the receiver.

The urgency in her sister's voice jolted her awake. "What's wrong, Darce? Are you okay? Is it Adam? Is he asking where I am?" They had told their brother that The Griffin management was sending her to a compulsory health and safety seminar down in Reno and she had to stay overnight.

"No, he's fine, don't worry," Darcey assured her. "But it's ... well, do you have a TV? Never mind. Give me second, and then check your messages."

"Check my messages?" But Darcey had already hung up. What the heck did her sister mean?

Two seconds later, her notifications lit up with a message from Darcey. Actually, there were dozens and dozens of messages piling up in her inbox.

Thea: *Where are you? Why aren't you answering my messages?*

Cathy: *How could you keep this from me? I thought we were friends!*

Stephanie: *OMG, you're all over the news!*

There were a couple more cryptic ones from other people at work, and some acquaintances she hadn't heard from in years. *What the heck was going on?*

Swiping the notifications away, she opened the latest message from Darcey. It was a link to a well-known gossip news site. "What the—" After clicking it, she realized what had sent Darcey into a tizzy.

Hero Ranger Who Saved VP—Married!?

There was a picture of her taken from an old social media

profile and one of her and Daniel as they walked out of the Rangers Headquarters building, his arm around her as she pressed to his side. Scrolling down, she began to read.

Daniel Rogers, dashing ranger who captured the hearts of America.... She skipped the next few lines that recapped the assassination attempt story until she saw her name. *Update: The mysterious Mrs. Rogers's identity has now been revealed: Sarah Mendez of Las Vegas, Nevada. According to their marriage certificate, they were wed three months ago at the Chapel of Hearts in Las Vegas. Ms. Mendez is a waitress at The Griffin Resort and Casino, as well as a lingerie designer. She sells her original creations on her own website, Silk, Lace, and Whispers.*

"How the hell did they figure that out?" she burst out.

Except for Darcey and the bank, no one knew about her side business, not even Adam or her friends at the casino. She deliberately didn't put her real name on the company site or social media accounts. Her real-life clients only knew her first name and ordered directly by text messaging her.

Silk, Lace, and Whispers wasn't a secret, per se, and designing lingerie was her passion, but when she decided to start up SLW, she'd had to think of Adam. He was a teenager, after all, and he was already getting teased and bullied at school being so ... different from his peers. The last thing he needed was for his classmates to find out his sister sold trashy underwear to strippers. The Summerlin boutique would have been far enough from his school district that none of his classmates would know about it, plus Darcey would be the one running the shop. And if her brick and mortar location took off, she'd be able to afford so many more things for Adam, including sending him to MIT, his dream college by the time he graduated. But now—

The phone rang again, making her jump to her feet.

"Sarah, are you there?" Darcey asked when she answered.

"Yeah, Darce, I'm here," she whispered. "Is it bad? Does Adam know yet?"

"He didn't say anything during breakfast."

"But he's going to find out." She buried her face in one hand. "Darce, this is awful."

"Awful?" Darcey chuckled. "Oh my God, Sarah, this is *great*."

"Great?"

"Yeah, why do you think I called? The orders on the SLW website are pouring in. That gossip rag linked back to us, and now we're down to half our inventory! At this rate, I'm going to have to put in an order to the manufacturer to replenish our stocks by lunchtime."

"Holy—you're not shitting me, are you?"

"No, I'm not. Really. The site crashed this morning—and boy, was that a nightmare—but I fixed it. I also asked Agnes for the day off just so I can handle the orders coming in. She's furious, but if this keeps up, I might be able to quit by the end of the month."

She chewed on her lip. "Really?"

"Really. Like, Sarah, we might not even need a loan from the bank at this rate. They'll be begging to give *us* money."

"Jesus." She sank back down on the lumpy bed. "I ... I need to think about this."

"Think about what?"

Though she hesitated for a moment, she told Darcey what happened with Daniel Rogers and his proposition.

"Oh my God," Darcey exclaimed. "What are you going to do?"

"Go home and help you with the orders, I guess," she said. "And file those annulment papers." If Daniel was true to his word, they would be waiting for her at the reception.

"Good God, Sarah, why would you do that now?"

"That's what I came here to do."

"Yeah but … couldn't you wait for a bit? Or even consider Daniel's offer?"

"You mean, be his fake wife? Why?"

"So you can milk this publicity for a bit longer. Any other brand would *kill* for this free advertising. The SLW social media accounts are getting thousands of followers. We might reach a million by end of the week. You can't buy this kind of publicity. If you just wait a few days, then the press'll find another thing to distract them, then you can come home and file the annulment quietly."

She gnawed at her lip. Could she really do it? Use Daniel like that? Well, technically, he was getting something out of this too. *Plus, he suggested faking their relationship in the first place.*

"If you won't do it for our business, do it for Adam," Darcey said.

"What do you mean? We can't lie to him. Not when this is all over the news."

"I'll explain to him what happened, okay? But think of the scandal and gossip that'll spread when it comes out you guys were strangers and got married while drunk? He'll get teased and bullied even more than he already is. However, if you let the press think you and Daniel are actually married for real and for love, no one will bat an eye. They'll even think it's romantic, and not some sordid tale of a drunken weekend in Vegas."

Darcey had a point, she conceded. Adam would probably get angry at her for being irresponsible, but then a good cover story would protect him publicly. "I'll think about it," she said. "And talk to Daniel."

"Daniel, huh?" Darcey asked in a teasing tone. "First name basis already. What's he like?"

Utterly handsome. Dazzling. Charming. Confident. There

was also a true strength in him she could sense. He felt solid, like a tree standing up to a storm. "He's fine, I guess."

"So, there's a possibility you won't be driving back today, huh? It's already ten there, right?"

Glancing at the clock, she realized her sister was right and that she'd overslept. "Crap." Rising to her feet, she stretched her arms out and let out a yawn. "All right, Darce, I should get my day started and find my future ex-husband. Just ... take care okay? And tell Adam—"

"I'll take care of Adam," she assured her. Darcey had always been the more maternal of the two them. Not that she didn't get along with Adam, but he and Sarah were so alike, they often clashed, especially now that he was a snotty teenager who thought he knew everything. Darcey was a soothing balm between them, the buffer that stopped them from exploding at each other all the time. "Go take care of business."

After putting the phone down, she took a shower, dried off and got dressed in a clean white blouse and yesterday's jeans, then headed to the reception. Sure enough, there was an envelope at the front desk with her name written on the front in neat handwriting. "I'll need to extend another night," she told the clerk at the desk. "Is that possible?"

"Of course, should I just charge your card?" he asked.

She gulped, remembering that that particular card was nearly maxed out. Actually, all her cards were, but if what Darcey was saying was true, then it shouldn't be an issue. "Yes, please. Thank you," she said before heading out to the parking lot and to her car.

It was another gorgeous summer day in the mountains, and she drove more leisurely this time, allowing herself to enjoy the views as she drove up to the Blackstone Rangers Headquarters. Thankfully, the news vans were nowhere in sight, but there were still a lot of people waiting outside. Ignoring them, she got out of her car and hurried to the entrance.

"I'm sorry, miss," the young man guarding the door said, holding a hand up. "I can't let you inside. If you're looking to get a hiking or camping permit, that's all done online and the entrance to the trails and campsites are down the road."

"I'm not," she answered. "I need to get inside and see Daniel Rogers."

The guard's mouth twisted ruefully. "You and everyone else." He nodded at the crowd gathered. "Why don't you join your friends, and maybe when Daniel comes out, he'll let you take a selfie with him?"

"That's not why I'm here." Her patience was running thin. "I'm his—"

"What's going on here, Reynolds?" someone said from behind.

"Hey, Russel," the guard greeted, then rolled his eyes. "Chief posted me here to keep the Rogers groupies away."

"I'm not a groupie," she said indignantly.

"Excuse me, I need to get in—oh, it's you."

Sarah looked up at the man who'd arrived, recognizing him as the blond ranger from the pie shop yesterday, though he was wearing street clothes today. "Hey. Thanks for the help yesterday. But I have to see Daniel. Now."

"You didn't see him yesterday? Didn't Anders help you out?"

"He did, and I saw Daniel. But ... I need to talk to him again." She cursed herself for being rude to this guy yesterday. "Um, maybe you could just give him my number?"

Clear blue eyes regarded her. "All right," he said. "You can let her in."

"But—"

"I'll take it up with the chief," he said, pushing past

Reynolds and holding the door open. "Let's go in. He's probably out patrolling, but I can find out what time he's swinging back to check in."

"Thank you," she said as she followed him inside. "I'm Sarah, by the way. I'm sorry if I was rude to you yesterday."

He flashed her a bright smile. "You're fine. I'm Gabriel, by the way. Gabriel Russel."

"Nice to meet you."

"Are you ... okay? Do you want a drink of water? Bathroom?" There was an odd look on his face.

"Er, I'm fine. I just need to see Daniel."

"Of course. We can go to the comms room and get someone to radio him. Meanwhile, I can get you a snack or maybe find a quiet place for you to sit down?"

Why the hell was this man—a stranger—obsessed with her comfort? "It's fine."

"Are you sure? I can get you some juice—oh, wait, there he is." Gabriel nodded up ahead.

She followed his gaze, to the two figures walking down towards them. Sure enough, she recognized Daniel's tall and broad form. However, hot emotion stabbed through her chest when she realized the other figure with him was female and stood a little too close to him for her liking. In fact, she didn't like anything about the girl next to him—not the way she bent her head close to him as they spoke or how she suddenly laughed and patted him on the shoulder when he said something.

"Sarah?" Gabriel asked.

But she ignored him as she marched toward the two of them, her hands curling into fists at her sides.

"Oh my God, Dan!" The blonde woman giggled again, and this time squeezed Daniel's bicep. "You're, like, so funny."

"I was just—Sarah?" The silvery blue gaze grew wide as they landed on her. "What are you doing here?"

Sarah felt the blonde's stare, but ignored it. "Hey, Daniel. Got a second?" *For your wife*, she almost added. It might have been worth it to say it out loud and see that bimbo's reaction.

"Of course. Listen, Carli," he said, turning to the blonde. "I'll talk to you later, okay?"

Carli's nostrils flared as her gaze flickered to Sarah's. "Yeah, I guess so. You'll have to tell me more about that fishing story. Maybe you could take me to that spot sometime. You know how much I love fishing. Bye now," she said with a sweet smile, before sauntering away.

Sarah gritted her teeth, trying to stop herself from ... from ... well, she wasn't sure what she wanted to do exactly, only that it involved something that would wipe the smirk from Carli's face.

"Sarah?" Daniel's voice broke through her thoughts. "Is there something the matter? Did I not sign the papers correctly?"

"You did," she admitted. "But ... can we talk somewhere private?"

"I ..." He looked confused but shrugged. "All right. Let's go to my cubicle."

He led her further down the hallway, then opened the door at the end, letting her go in first. They headed to one of the empty cubicles. "Do you want some coffee? Or tea?"

"I'm fine," she said. "I'm sure you're wondering what I'm doing here." Her throat felt dry and her palms were sweaty. God, why was she nervous?

"Kinda. But I don't mind," he added quickly. "I mean ... uh ..." He rubbed the back of his neck. "I thought you'd be on your way back to Vegas by now."

"Yeah, I overslept and ... wait, you haven't seen any of the news sites?"

"News sites?" He shook his head. "I came in early today to, uh, do some paperwork. So, I haven't checked my phone. Hold on." Circling the table, he grabbed the phone on the side table. "Is it more stuff about the VP and—oh." His eyes scanned the screen quickly. "Shit. Fuck." Tossing the phone down, he slammed his palms on the tabletop. "I'm sorry, Sarah. I didn't mean for this to get out of hand. Maybe Damon is right, and I should issue a statement to the press, tell them to leave you alone. Then we can file the annulment—"

"No!" she protested, then bit her lip. "I mean, don't issue a statement asking the press to leave me alone. That'll have the opposite effect." Her heart drummed at the thought of what she wanted to say next. "And as for the annulment ... maybe ... perhaps ... we can hold off just for a bit. At least until the attention dies down."

His head snapped up. "Hold on. Are you saying we should stay married?"

"Uh, yeah. I mean ... I thought about what you said." Her hands wrung together. "I think it would be best if we could keep certain details about our wedding from leaking out."

"You mean, about us getting drunk?" he asked sheepishly.

"Yeah. The thing is, I have to protect my family, you know? I mean, I don't want them to bear the brunt because I made one mistake."

His shoulders stiffened. "Mistake?" he said in a low voice.

"Yes," she said. "And I'm sure you ... I mean, what would your family think if they find out you got drunk and then married a stranger?"

"I ..." He let out a low grunt. "I guess you have a point. I haven't even thought of them. I mean, I said I'd tell my dad about it, but I read the papers and they seemed legit. Didn't seem like there was a point in letting my parents know." His brows snapped together. "I really am sorry that the press is dragging your name through the mud."

She chuckled nervously. "It's fine. I mean, if anything, I'm getting some free publicity for my business." She hoped she had mentioned that casually enough.

"But what about your boyfriend?"

"Boyfriend?" she asked, puzzled.

"I asked you if there was someone else and you didn't answer. I assumed you were dating someone."

"I didn't say I was," she said. "So you don't have to worry about a jealous lover or anything. But if you changed your mind—"

"No," he interrupted. "I haven't."

"But so ... how should we go about this? I've never faked being married before. Or real married either."

The smile on his face lit up the room. "I guess the first thing we need to do is explain how it is we got married in secret. How about—"

The office door flew open behind them, interrupting Daniel. "Well, look what we have here."

Whirling her head around, she saw Anders standing in the doorway.

"Hey, Rogers," he greeted, then nodded at Sarah as a shit-eating grin spread across his face. "Mrs. Rogers."

"Anders, you asshole!" Gabriel skidded behind Anders, pushing him into the office. "Sorry, Daniel," he said sheepishly. "I tried to stop him, but this fucker's too fast." He looked at Sarah apologetically. "Sorry."

Anders burst out laughing. "Oh my God, you should see your fucking face, Rogers. What's the matter? Are the bonds of matrimony strangling your neck already?"

"Matrimony?" Gabriel's jaw dropped. "What is he saying?"

Daniel's face was red, and a vein strained at his neck. "Get the fuck outta here, Stevens, before I break *your* fucking face."

"Jeez, so touchy," Anders said, rolling his eyes.

"What's going on Daniel?" Gabriel asked.

"Nothing," Daniel answered. "Just get out of here."

"Wait, you don't know?" Anders looked at Gabriel.

"Know what?"

Anders shook his head. "Remember that little trip to Vegas three months ago? When our man Rogers here disappeared, he didn't just hook up with little miss inked goddess here. He also married her."

"You got *married*?" Gabriel exclaimed. "I thought you just got her pregnant!"

"Pregnant?" Sarah sputtered. "You thought I was ..." No wonder he kept trying to make her comfortable. "I'm not pregnant." She slapped a hand on her forehead. "I can't believe I've had to say that twice in twenty-four hours."

"What the hell is going on here?"

All three men went stiff as a board.

The man who walked inside the office filled the room with his mere presence. He was tall, dark-haired, and there was something menacing about him that Sarah just couldn't explain. His bright green gaze bore right into her with a laser-like precision.

"Chief," Daniel began, his tone deferential. "I can explain."

"Who's this, and why is she in here? This area is for employees only," he said.

"I'm sure you can give her a pass," Daniel said. "After all, she's my wife."

A thrill ran down her spine at the possessive way he said those words. The chief, on the other hand, went slack-jawed.

"Wife?"

"I can explain. Maybe we should go into your office?"

Daniel suggested. "If you give me a few minutes, I can get Sarah settled."

The chief composed himself. "Fine. I'll see you in five—ten minutes." Turning on his heel, he walked away.

Anders chortled. "I've never seen him so—"

"Buzz off," Daniel ordered. "Now."

"But—"

"C'mon." Gabriel hooked an arm around his. "Let's go." Ignoring Anders's protests, he dragged him out of the office.

"I'm sorry," Daniel said. "I'm really sorry about this mess."

"There was no way this was going to be easy," she said. "That was your boss, right? Are you going to be okay? Will he fire you?"

"For having you in here? Nah. His wife comes by all the time." He grinned sheepishly. "But I do have a full workday ahead of me. I could try to get out early and—"

"No, please. Don't take off work on my account."

"All right. But we should talk. Do you want to stay here for a bit? Or go back to your motel?"

The thought of going out there and facing the people waiting outside did not sit well with her. "Would you mind if I, uh, stayed here while you met your boss? And use your computer? I need to check my email." Since she was going to stay here for a while, she might as well get some work done and have Darcey overnight her some of her stuff, like her tablet PC where she did all her work.

"No, go ahead." He gestured to the chair behind the desk. "Take all the time you need. If you're hungry, there's a cafeteria outside." An awkward silence hung between them. "I'll go talk to Damon, and then I'll come back and we can figure this out."

"Sure," she said as she sat down on the leather office chair.

"I'll see you. I won't be long."

"Okay."

He hesitated for a moment, then turned on his heel. When the door closed behind him, she let out a sigh. *Focus, Sarah.* She had decided to go on with this farce for her business and her family, so she had to think of the end goal. With that in mind, she called Darcey.

"Hey, Darce, it's me. Everything okay?"

"Uh-huh. Whew!" It sounded like she plopped down on the couch. "The manufacturer got back to me and said they can push our delivery up, and we can have the stock next week. And I'm getting ready to start packing all the stuff and sending them out."

"Great, but we're fresh out of what we have on the site?"

"'Fraid so," Darcey said. "But we do have the new collection in the storage locker."

"I wasn't planning to have that out until fall." Sarah bit her lip. "It's not ready to go on the site yet. I haven't even photographed the samples."

"Yeah, but next week might be too late," her sister replied. "We've got nothing to sell, and our social media's getting flooded with messages and comments. I've put up 'sold out' graphics and everything, but people are still wanting more."

Sarah wanted to kick herself for this lost opportunity. If she had an actual store, it wouldn't have been a problem keeping extra stock. "All right. Can you send me a couple samples from the fall collection? Overnight it to me. And I'll need my tablet, some clothes and a couple of things, too. I'll message you a list and give you the address to my motel."

"I'm heading out for some packing material so I'll get that out right away."

"Thanks, Darce."

Am I doing the right thing, she thought as she hung up. Everything happened fast and soon she was the one propositioning him to stay married, and now, here she was. How did one fake a marriage anyway? Would this even work? What if someone discovered this was all a lie?

Don't concern yourself with that. Growing up the way she did, there was no use in thinking of all the bad things that could happen, because at some point or another, something bad would happen anyway. It was better to live in the moment. But hopefully, none of this would blow up in her face.

Chapter 5

Daniel didn't want to leave Sarah all alone in the office. Hell, his bear didn't want to leave her, *at all.* But her coming here was a surprise—a pleasant one, but a surprise nonetheless—and it was like his world was thrown off its axis.

God, she was even more beautiful than yesterday. The white linen top she wore went up to her neck but left her arms bare, making her skin seem like golden bronze and the stained glass tattoo stand out even more. Her hair was pulled back in a high, sleek ponytail that fell behind her like a glossy waterfall.

He didn't expect to see her today. Heck, he didn't expect to see her ever again. Though his entire being—not to mention his inner bear—fought with him as he looked over the papers and signed them, he knew it was the right thing to do. He thought it would be easy to convince her to stay married, even coming up with the harebrained excuse of needing her to keep over-amorous women away.

But, mate or not, Sarah was a real-life person, who had a life before him. It was physically painful to think that there was someone else in her life. She didn't confirm it, but didn't deny it either, but it sounded like there was someone else that she cared deeply about. And while the thought of that made him want to tear something apart, he had to respect that she was her own person and that even though she was his fated mate, he couldn't just take something that belonged to someone else first.

Now, here she was, like fate dropped her in his lap—again. She wasn't attached, a fact that made his heart nearly burst out of his chest. Which meant he could still find a way to woo her and make her stay and be his mate. He didn't want to blow this chance to show her they were meant to be together.

But first ... He glanced down the hallway, in the direction of Damon's office. He had to take care of this first. Not sure what he was going to say to his friend and boss, he straightened his shoulders and strode toward the chief's office.

Being the type of person who preferred to rip off a Band-Aid, he grabbed the door handle, yanked it open and strode inside. "Chief, first of all let me—what the hell are you all doing here?"

It wasn't just Damon in the office, but Gabriel and Anders were there as well, standing by Damon's massive oak desk. "Chief, I need to talk to you, *alone*."

"Were you going to mention your wife at all?" Damon asked, hands folding over his chest.

"It's not what you think," he said.

"Why don't you sit down and explain." Damon waved him over and motioned for him to sit. "Let's talk. As friends. What's going on?"

His instinct was to turn around and run; this was his workplace after all, and Damon was his boss. But he reminded himself that he had gone through the punishing training camp with these three men, and they had forged a bond no one else would understand. So, he walked over and sank down on the chair. "She's mine," he said with a sigh. "My mate."

"Sarah?" Gabriel gaped. "Your wife? She's your mate?"

"Jesus." Damon looked flabbergasted.

"Fuck me," Anders moaned. "Not you, too. All right, I'm out." He threw his hands up in the air and pivoted on his heel, walking toward the door.

"Where the hell are you going?" Gabriel called. But the door had already slammed shut, and the tiger shifter was gone.

"Leave him alone," Damon said. "You know how he is about women." He turned back to Daniel. "So, you married your mate."

"That's kinda like cheating, isn't it?" Gabriel asked. "I mean I had to kidnap a gnome to get Temperance to go out with me. And we only got engaged last night."

"What do you mean *kidnap a gnome*?" Daniel asked.

"He'll explain later. But, hey, congrats, man." Damon clapped the lion shifter on the back and pulled him in for a quick hug.

"Thanks. I came here to tell you, but then I ran into Sarah." Gabriel's golden brows furrowed together. "So, Rogers, tell us what happened."

"I'm not really sure. I can't remember," Daniel said sheepishly. "But here's what I think did happen." He told them about the night of the bachelor party, how he was drugged by the guy who was harassing the stripper. "I drank the gin and tonic, and then ... I must have bumped into Sarah. Their group was next to us at The Pink Palace. She remembers that much at least. We left and then ... it was kind of a blur from there for both of us. I remember bits and pieces." His cheeks warmed at the flashes of tawny skin and sweet, plush lips. "We must have gone to the chapel at some point. And then I woke up alone at the motel."

"Only you would get drugged, then marry someone, Rogers," Gabriel said with a chuckle. "But you gotta admit, it makes it easier to convince her to be with you." He paused. "I mean, that's what you want, right?"

"Of course it is!" His grizzly gnashed its teeth at the implication they would want anyone else. "But ... she came here to ask me for an annulment." He continued his story of how Sarah showed up yesterday and asked him to sign the papers and he tried convincing her to keep up the charade. "She said no, of course, but then she came here this morning to tell me she changed her mind. Something about protecting her family and her business." He was still confused about it, but he wasn't about to let this chance get away.

"So, what are you going to do now?" Damon asked.

"Well, I was hoping you guys could help me out. I mean, you two are mated to humans. What do I do?"

Damon and Gabriel looked at each other, a silent communication passing between them. Finally, Gabriel spoke up. "There isn't any formula or steps in claiming your mate."

"It was different for me," Damon said. "I fought with my bear because I didn't think I deserved Anna Victoria. I tried keeping her away, but I ended up hurting myself and her."

That definitely sounded like the closed-off, broody chief. Still, Daniel saw the changes that Damon had gone through after meeting his mate, and he was happy that the chief was finally living his life to the fullest.

"And I went after Temperance the moment I met her, but she didn't want anything to do with me at first. Not because she had anything against being mates, in fact, she pretty much accepted it once I told her." Knowing Gabriel, he probably pushed and shoved his way into his mate's life until she relented.

But Sarah was nothing like Temperance and Anna Victoria, so it was obvious he was going to have to figure this out.

"Don't let her go, man," Gabriel continued. "Do what you

need to do to keep her. She's human, but she seems like a smart girl. She wants to stay married for show? Use that to your advantage. Keep her close, get to know her."

"And let her get to know you." Damon's tone turned serious. "Daniel, speaking as your friend and not just your boss, you're a catch. Any girl would be lucky to have you as their mate."

"You just have to convince her," Gabriel said. "And something tells me she won't make it easy."

"They usually don't," Damon added with a snort. "But it's all worth it, when you bond."

A blissful look passed on both men's faces, and Daniel's gut twisted in envy. This was what he was waiting for his whole life, right? To find the other half of his soul and have a relationship just like his parents had?

"So," Gabriel said. "What are you going to do?"

"She and I need to sit down and talk," he said. "Work out what we're supposed to do."

"Take her to dinner," Gabriel urged. "Giorgio's. I'll make the reservations for seven tonight."

"I know you didn't want to take the time off," Damon said. "But if you need to take off early, do it."

"Thanks, guys," he said. "I'll keep that in mind."

He left Damon's office and walked back to his own. Sarah was still at his desk, typing away at the computer. Sensing his presence, she looked up. "You're back."

His heart squeezed in his chest at how gorgeous she was. "Yeah. Um, don't worry, I worked it out with my boss. He said take any time I need."

Dark brown brows snapped together. "For what?"

"To, uh, work out our situation. He's been urging me to at least make a statement of some kind to get the press off my back." He walked in and sat on the chair opposite her. "I have to get some work done outside for a couple of hours before I can clock out. If you want, you can stay here or meet me for dinner tonight."

"Dinner?" A dark brow rose suspiciously. "Like a *date*?"

"Just a meal," he said quickly. "So we can talk about what this arrangement will entail. Seven o'clock at Giorgio's on Main Street."

She nodded, seemingly buying his explanation. "Sounds fair. I'll go back to my motel." Getting up from the chair, she walked around the table. He got up, too, at the same time, but the cubicle was so small that they bumped into each other as they both tried to get out at the same time.

"Oops!" She bounced back, but he caught her, snaking his arm around her waist and pulling her to him.

His entire body tensed as his heart began to race at their closeness. There was something familiar about this, the way her curves fit into his body and her sweet scent teasing him. For a moment, he could swear he saw the recognition in her eyes, too, but she quickly pushed away from him.

"Sorry," she murmured, brushing past him.

Damn it! "I'll walk you to your car."

"N-no!" she protested, then cleared her throat. "Too many people outside, they'll see you," she added. "I'll slip out as quickly as I can."

As the door closed behind her, he expelled a long-held breath. "Fuck." He plopped back down on the chair, raking his hands through his hair. His bear roared at him, pressing him to claim and bond their mate now.

From what Gabriel and Damon said, it sounded like it wasn't so simple. And Sarah had to want it, too, of course. He supposed if they had done this in the right order, it would have been easier. He could court her, date her, and their feelings would eventually develop. Now, he had to convince her to actually stay married, and accept their bond.

He wasn't going to give up, not now. She was his to lose, and he wasn't going to let her go without a fight.

Daniel had never felt so nervous in his life. The rest of his shift seemed to stretch on, and the tension in his chest grew so much he thought he would burst by the time he was finally driving down to Main Street. There was no time to go home and get dressed, but he always kept a nice outfit in his locker at work. *You never know when you'll need to get all dressed up*, Dad had always said. He was glad he had taken that advice to heart.

After parking his truck in the back of Giorgio's, he walked to the front entrance. He was five minutes early, so he waited by the hostess station. Sure enough, at seven on the dot, the door opened, and Sarah stepped inside.

His heart nearly burst out of his chest at the sight of his mate. She was still wearing the same outfit, though he noticed her lips were glossy, and her hair was down in waves around her gorgeous face. Their eyes met, though she quickly turned away, glancing around her. "Nice place."

Giorgio's was a classic Italian restaurant, complete with dark paneling walls, cozy booths, and low lighting. It was pretty much where Blackstone's couples had all their romantic dates.

"Uh, yeah, a friend made the reservation," he said. "I hope you're hungry. The food here is good."

The hostess led them to their table, and Daniel groaned inwardly. It was one of the corner booths, away from prying eyes, lit up by a simple centerpiece of candles. Three red roses were arranged on the table, while a scattering of petals dotted the white linen cloth.

"Just a meal, right?" Sarah said wryly as she slid into the booth.

Damn it. He should have taken her to the diner like he'd originally planned. Gabriel had done a good job, but he didn't want to scare Sarah away. "Of course." He flashed her an innocent smile.

After scanning the menu, they gave their orders to their waiter. As soon as he was gone, Daniel spoke up.

"So how was—"

"Did you—"

They both stopped, and an edgy silence hung between them. "Go ahead," he said.

"No, you go."

"No, ladies first," he urged.

"Do people still say that?" she chuckled.

"I've been told I'm old-fashioned." He grinned at her. "But I think old-fashioned is good, especially these days."

"Is that so?" She smirked at him. "No wonder you proposed right away."

"Hey now." He put his hands up. "How do you know *you* weren't the one to ask me to marry you?"

She cackled. "Ha! As if."

Seeing her laugh and smile made his insides turn to mush. "I'll have you know; I don't marry on the first date. I have a three-date rule before matrimony."

"Then it must have been me," she conceded. "I have been known to propose to any man I come across."

The tension in the air broke, but before Daniel could say anything else, the waiter came back with their drinks and a basket of bread with Giorgio's signature strawberry balsamic dip. He was thinking of a way to get back to their banter when she spoke up.

"So," she began as she put her glass down after taking a sip of her sparkling water. "We should probably talk about our arrangement."

"Yeah." His heart plummeted but he continued. "What did you have in mind?"

"So, I was thinking about our backstory."

"Backstory?"

"Yeah. About how we met and stuff. And how we wound up married."

"And?"

"It sounds cliched, but the most logical explanation would be that we met on the Internet. A dating site or app or something."

"Ah, that makes sense," he said. "We could say we started chatting over a year ago, and then I came to visit you."

"Exactly. And we were doing the long-distance thing," she added.

"My job ties me here," he said. "I can't exactly be a ranger out on The Strip."

"And mine keeps me in Vegas. But we see each other every few weeks."

"And the wedding?"

Her nose wrinkled. "I haven't thought that far ahead yet."

"Hmm." He scratched at his head. "How about ... I was in Vegas for Damon's bachelor party, and I was so overwhelmed with emotion and tired of the long distance that I impulsively asked you to marry me, and you said yes."

"Hmm." She tapped a finger on her chin. "I guess that could work. And we've been keeping it secret because ..."

"Because I didn't want to overshadow Damon's wedding," he said. "And it's not really a secret. We just ... didn't tell anyone until we figured out who was going to move where."

"Right." She worried at her lip. "Okay, now we should figure out how long this arrangement will last. I can't stay here in Blackstone forever."

His bear chuffed, but he told it to pipe down. "Of course. How about two weeks?"

"I was thinking more of three days. I can go home on the weekend."

"Oh." His heart plummeted. "Why just three days?"

"First of all, I can't really afford to stay in that motel for too long, plus, I have to get back to Vegas to take care of my business. Three more days should be enough to convince reporters and your 'fans' that our marriage is real and this is how our relationship works. Then when I leave, we could just ... let it die a natural death. If anyone asks, we should just tell them it didn't work out. Maybe we could say this was the week we were working on our marriage, and we decided to split up."

Just the thought of her leaving made his stomach clench. "Sounds like a good plan," he forced himself to say. "But there's one flaw there."

Her gaze narrowed. "And what's that?"

"You can't stay at the motel the entire time," he pointed out. "That doesn't make sense, if we're really married."

"I—" Her mouth closed shut and she slumped back. "Then what do you suggest?"

"Move in with me."

Her brows snapped together. "*Excuse me*?"

"You heard me," he said. "Stay with me, and then you don't have to worry about paying for the motel."

"Stay with you? At your place?" she asked incredulously. "Where would I sleep?"

"Er ... I'm renovating my parents' house. I'm still working on it but it's got five bedrooms, so take your pick." It would only take him a couple of hours to get the place livable again. "It's not like anyone will know if we don't sleep in the same room."

She shook her head. "No, I can't," she said. "We'll just have to be careful. It's not like those reporters follow you around day and night, right? And it's been days since you rescued the VP. Once we make a statement to the press, they'll leave us alone. In fact, that's probably what we should do first thing. We can write it up tonight and read it out to the press tomorrow."

Unfortunately, he couldn't think of anything else to counter her argument. *Fuck.* He had three days to convince her to stay, and they wouldn't even be spending a lot of time together. But before he could even say anything, their waiter came back with their food.

"This looks delicious," Sarah said.

"Yeah." But with the churning in his stomach, food was the last thing he needed right now.

"Enjoy your meal," the waiter said before he left.

As they ate, they made small talk about the food and the weather, but they avoided any more talk about their arrangement. When the check came, he grabbed the black folder from the waiter before he put it down.

"How much is my half?" she asked.

"Half?" He frowned. "I told you, I owe you dinner."

"Nonsense," she made a grab for the folder, but he held it away from her. "C'mon Daniel, just give me the damned thing."

An idea popped into his head. "I will," he began. "If you at least come with me tonight and see the house."

Her gaze narrowed at him. "Seriously?"

He wasn't sure why he was asking her to do this, but it seemed like the right move. *Anything to keep the evening going.* There was no way he was going to admit defeat. If he only had three days with her, then he was going to make sure they would stick together. "It's not far from here, and all I'm asking is for you to look at the house and see how big it is. We might not even run into each other."

"So, you want me to come and see your big house, huh?" she asked, a hint of humor in her tone.

Was she making an innuendo? He swallowed hard. "Uh-huh. You'll have your choice of bedrooms, your own bathroom, and we even have a pool and hot tub."

"We?"

"Yeah. It's my parents' house, but they live in Texas now, and they left it to me to renovate and update. So." He shook the black folder at her. "What do you say?"

"Fine." She snatched the folder from him. "Let's pay and get out of here."

She put in a couple of bills into the folder and he did the same, then they walked out to the parking lot.

"Just follow me, okay?" He waited for her to get into her car before heading toward his truck. Turning the engine on, he maneuvered out his parking space, then out of the lot. For a moment, he thought she would change her mind and drive in the opposite direction, but when he turned into the street, her headlights popped into his rearview mirror.

With a sigh of relief, he continued out toward the highway. He wasn't sure why he asked her to some see the house. But somehow, it felt right. Like he wanted her to see this place he had been fixing up for the last year. *For her*.

It clicked in his mind all of a sudden. This home he'd been working on, with his own two hands, was all for her, his mate. He wanted so bad to see her live in it. With him. Have their children grow up there and—

The loud *kaboom* came from nowhere and jolted him out of his thoughts. The world flipped over several times and he realized that sound came from his truck. Metal crashed and scraped on asphalt, making his sensitive eardrums ring. Closing his eyes and gnashing his teeth, his first thought was of Sarah, who had been a few feet behind him.

When the ringing in his ears dissipated, he opened his eyes. The truck was on its side and there was a gaping hole in the windshield where the glass had shattered. Gasoline burned his nostrils as he felt the temperature rise. He knew he had to get out of there *now*.

He unsheathed a claw and sliced through his seat belt, then crawled out of the cab, getting as far away from the truck as possible. His vehicle was completely trashed, but that wasn't important right now. *Something was definitely wrong*.

The hairs on the back of his neck rose and his grizzly tensed before letting out a warning growl. It was eerily quiet outside, and as his shifter vision adjusted to the darkness, he saw six figures approaching him. His inner bear raised its paws, ready to attack. There was something about them that made his brain scream danger, and considering he turned into a nine foot, eight hundred pound killing machine, he knew there was more to those men than meets the eye. They all wore black and were fully armed with several kinds of automatic weapons.

"Who the hell are you?" he said, standing up to full height, ready to shift at any moment.

One of them, a tall man with a shock of white hair and pale silver eyes, spoke. "You damned filthy beasts are hard to kill."

He gnashed his teeth. *Damn anti-shifters*. But, how did they get his truck to flip over?

And more, important, where was Sarah?

It took all his might not to turn around and check for her. These men were focused on him for now and he needed to keep it that way. "What do you want?"

"You, Daniel Rogers," the man replied. "Specifically, we want you *dead*." The others around him moved closer and began to raise their weapons.

"I'd like to see you try." Clothes ripped and bones snapped as he shifted into his grizzly. The mighty beast roared, its massive arms raising high, claws extending from furry paws. There were more of them, but he was a shifter and thus he had superior speed, strength and healing. He went for the man with the largest weapon and brought his paws down on him, raking his razor-sharp claws down his body, piercing through the body armor he wore.

The human let out a scream, and his companions all pointed their weapons at them. Daniel's grizzly slammed its body sideward, knocking down two more of his attackers.

"Get him!" someone screamed.

The hulking bear got to its feet, ready to attack as it saw the weapons raised.

"No!"

The feminine shout made his blood run cold. *Fuck!* He was hoping Sarah had run away when his truck flipped over. She must have come up on them.

He heard the sound of the trigger pulling, and the bear let out a roar. Daniel braced himself for the pain, but it didn't come. Instead, he felt something heavy wrap around his bear and force it down. They had deployed some kind of metal net that engulfed the animal's body.

"Daniel!" Sarah was running straight toward them now, seemingly unaware of the danger she was in.

Run away! He screamed from inside his bear, but it was no use. His animal was in a rage, its claws tearing at the steel mesh. These men, whoever they were, weren't messing around.

"Grab the female," someone ordered. "We'll have to get rid of her too."

The grizzly roared in fury, but the net was too strong. Helpless, it watched as one of the men broke away and ran straight toward Sarah.

"Don't even try, you filthy animal," the white-haired man hissed. "That net was made for beasts like you."

"Why don't we just kill it now?" Someone interjected.

"You *know* why." Pale silver eyes full of hate trained on him. "We must wait."

"Just because he stopped Jones from killing Baker?"

"Shut up, idiot!"

"Sorry, boss."

"Get your hands off me, asshole!" Sarah shouted as one of the men dragged her forward. "What did you do to him?"

"Him?" The white-haired man mocked. "He's a filthy animal. Are you one of them too?"

"Fuck you—ow!" Sarah cried as the man holding her jerked her back.

White hot rage coursed through his veins, and the grizzly gathered all its strength and slashed at the net over and over again. Pain didn't even register in their brain, even as their claws chipped and tore from the attempt to escape. However, when its teeth caught in the net, the mesh gave way.

"Motherfucker! They said that thing would hold!"

"Get the tranqs ready! But put a bullet in his head if you have to."

"No! Don't kill him!"

"Take that bitch away!"

Daniel ignored them as the grizzly continued to chew and tear through the mesh. He could only focus on Sarah, her cries and screams as one of them tossed her over his shoulder. No, Daniel and his bear could only focus on one thing: their mate.

"Shoot! Shoot!"

There was a soft *pffft* sound from behind him and he felt the sting of a needle on his back. It only fueled their rage, and soon they were free of the net. Hopping onto its feet, the grizzly lunged toward Sarah.

"Imbeciles!" The white-haired man shrieked.

The grizzly lumbered forward, but its steps faltered. *Not*

now, Daniel raged. But the tranquilizer was already slowly making it was through their system.

"He's going down! Abomination! You—"

A loud screech pierced the air, interrupting the white-haired man's tirade.

"What the fuck is—"

"Jesus Christ Almigh—"

"—get out of here!"

The wind picked up around them, like a hurricane passing through. Daniel felt something *big* around them, a presence that he couldn't name. However, as his grizzly was falling over, it bent its head back toward the sky before it hit the ground.

Holy shit.

At first, he thought he'd hit his head too hard. But the air above him was definitely shimmering as something large appeared overhead. Something *very* large, with wings and a humungous snake-like body. Light rippled across green-gold scales as the creature let out another earth-shattering shriek.

What the fuck.

"What do we do, boss?" someone said. "That's a—"

"Dragon!"

Daniel blinked. Dragon? Was it Matthew or Jason Lennox? Had they seen the accident and swooped in to investigate? He'd only seen the twin dragons a few times in his life, but he remembered them clearly. And that snake-like dragon with the green and gold scales was neither of the Lennox siblings.

"Goddammit, not again!" The white-haired man hissed. "That meddling—"

The dragon swooped down low, its tail flicking on the ground like a whip as it approached them.

"Duck!" The men ran, scattering away. The creature beat its bat-like wings hard and flew up again.

Daniel could feel the effects of the tranquilizer ebbing away.

They must not have used a large enough dose. As his grizzly's body began to shrink, he closed his eyes, trying to speed up the change. When he was fully human, he shot to his feet.

"Daniel!"

Something hurtled toward him, and slim arms wrapped around his neck. He inhaled a familiar sweet scent, and his grizzly settled within in. Their mate was safe.

"Sarah," he rasped, pulling her close to him, her curves fitting into the hard planes of his body perfectly like interlocking pieces of a puzzle. "I thought they'd ... that I lost ..."

"That asshole who picked me up like a sack of potatoes dropped me as soon as he saw that ... that thing." She shivered, and he held her tighter. "God, when I saw your car flip over, I was so scared."

His chest filled with hope. She had been frightened for him. That meant she *cared.* "I was scared for you too," he admitted. "Sarah ..." He sighed and then buried his face in her hair. God, this was perfect. So perfect. He only had to turn his head and he could kiss her cheek, and then make his way to her lips.

The sound of an engine roaring to life and tires screeching made her pull away. "Oh my God, those men who tried to capture you!" She pointed behind him. "They're getting away!"

Turning his head, he saw the taillights of what was probably an SUV in the distance down the road. "It's all right. We're safe. You're safe," he said. He longed to pull her back into his arms, but the moment had passed.

"I don't understand." She shook her head. "What the hell is going on?"

"I—"

The wind picked up again, and every instinct in his head screamed as he felt that same looming presence around him again. "Stay behind me," he ordered, pulling Sarah to his back.

"What's going on?"

"It's back ... whatever it is."

"What—oh!" She sucked in a breath.

The ground shook, and she held onto his shoulder. The air shifted and shimmered again. He gritted his teeth, ready for the dragon to show up, but the green-gold creature didn't materialize. Instead, a human-like figure began to form in front of them. Behind him, Sarah gasped.

"Are you all right?"

Daniel blinked as the man's figure solidified. He was tall, nearly seven feet, with short-cropped dark blond hair and a thick beard, his bare arms decorated in rune-like tattoos. His torso and legs were covered in what appeared to be armor that mimicked his scales, and a large sword was strapped to his side. The man was literally and figuratively a knight in shining armor.

"Uh ... yeah?" He wasn't sure what to say. He was on their side, obviously, as he had chased those men away. "Who are you?"

"I know you are surprised, so allow me to introduce myself." He gave them a small nod. "My name is Thoralf, Former Captain of the Guard for Their Majesties, the King and Queen of the Northern Isles."

Northern Isles? Why did that sound familiar? His accent sounded Scandinavian, but he couldn't quite remember where he'd heard that name before. "Those men ..."

Golden brows slashed downward. "Ah, yes. I'd been in pursuit of them for days now, ever since I had heard they were taking some sort of action. I never thought, though, that they would come here for you, Daniel Rogers of the Blackstone Rangers."

"You know who I am?"

"Of course. You saved the life of an important man, a heroic deed reported of far and wide. And now it seems you have created enemies because of this. I—"

The sound of approaching vehicles interrupted Thoralf. Both he and Daniel tensed, ready to attack. The headlights grew bigger as they drew closer.

"If you take the female to safety, I shall take care of these blackguards," the dragon shifter said.

Daniel nodded. "You got it."

"What is going on?" Sarah asked.

Three SUVS stopped in front of them, cutting off their access to the road. That wouldn't be any trouble to Daniel, however, as he could shift into his grizzly and carry Sarah into the woods behind them.

"Get ready to grab onto me," he said.

"Grab on? What do you mean?"

A growl rattled from his chest as his bear readied itself for the change. Thoralf, too, was preparing as scales appeared on his bare arms. The SUV's doors opened, but only one man emerged from the leading vehicle.

"Don't attack, we're on your side!" The headlights covered the man in shadow but Daniel recognized the voice. "Daniel! Bro, it's me. Jason. Jason Lennox."

As the lights behind him clicked off, all the tension left Daniel's body. "Jason? What are you doing here?" Though he knew Jason—he was a year behind him in high school, but they had been on the football team together—he remained rooted to the spot, as the adrenaline was still coursing through his system, plus, his grizzly was feeling on edge with *two* dragons around him and their mate.

Jason Lennox jogged toward them. "We have regular patrols around town, and one of them reported a disturbance here." He skidded to a halt when his gaze landed on Thoralf. "Hey, don't I know you?"

"My lord!" Thoralf immediately sank to one knee. "Yes, it is I, Thoralf. Former Captain of the Guard for their Majesties, the King and Queen of the Northern Isles."

Jason looked flummoxed. "Aleksei didn't say anything about sending anyone here."

"I'm not here on any official capacity, my lord Jason," Thoralf began. "I am on a quest and it has led me here to Blackstone."

"Um, you can get up now, Thoralf," Jason said. "And you can just call me Jason."

"But, my lord, you are brother to Her Majesty, Queen Sybil of the Northern Isles, The Great Fire-breather, Daughter of the Blackstone Dragon, Duchess of Svartalheim, Lady of the Barents Islands, and—"

"You're in America now, Thoralf," Jason urged him to get up. "Please, no need for formalities."

"As you wish." Thoralf got to his feet.

Sybil? A lightbulb lit up in Daniel's head. Jason's youngest sibling, Sybil Lennox, had married some European prince last year. It was the talk of the town, especially that huge wedding they had in Blackstone. The entire town was invited, and Main Street had a huge block party to celebrate. He'd even stood on the sidewalk when the happy couple drove through town in a horse-drawn carriage.

"What's the heck is going on?"

Shit, he'd nearly forgotten about Sarah. "I'm not sure myself, to be honest," he said. "Jason? Do you know anything about the guys who attacked us?"

The dragon shifter sighed. "It's kind of a long story, plus, I do need to take you in to make a statement."

"Statement? Should we head down to the police department?"

"Er, not quite." He raked his hand through his hair. "I—oh."

His brows snapped together when he saw Sarah behind Daniel. "I didn't realize you weren't alone."

"Uh, yeah. This is Sarah," he introduced. "My wife." The words just rolled off his tongue naturally.

"I'm not!" she protested quickly. "I mean, I am. But I won't be soon."

Jason looked confused. "Oh, uh ... I don't need to know the details. But, yeah, we should explain a few things to you. Besides," he cocked his head toward his truck. Or rather, what was left of it. "You'll probably need a ride to town anyway."

Daniel groaned. "Fuck me." His truck was trashed.

"And some clothes?" Jason added, amused.

Did he forget that his clothes had ripped off when shifted? "Er, yeah."

It was dark, so maybe Sarah didn't notice. However, she shifted uncomfortably when he peeked at her, and she suddenly found something interesting in the distance.

"C'mon," Jason said. "We have some spare clothes in the truck."

"Thanks, man." He itched to ask Jason who "we" were in the first place, but he figured he'd find out soon enough.

Chapter 6

Sarah had never been so confused in her whole life. Sure, she was used to emotional rollercoasters, but not quite like this. Shock, fear, awe, panic, dread, and—much to her annoyance—lust, cycled through her in the span of ten minutes.

The moment she saw Daniel's truck hit with some kind of explosive and flip over, her heart leapt to her throat. She slammed on the brakes and watched from her car, frozen in place as she watched the truck land on its side; the sound of the crash of metal on asphalt was something she would never forget. She knew she should have called 911, but something snapped inside her when she saw those men threatening Daniel, so she got out to help him. In hindsight, it was an idiotic move because what the hell did she think she could do against half a dozen men wielding weapons?

Sure enough, they caught Daniel, then her, then that other guy—a freaking *dragon*—showed up. Thankfully he was on their side but he literally appeared from nowhere. She didn't even know shifters could do that, as Darcey never just materialized in front of her.

And now, after what seemed like a very men-in-black

conspiracy theory turn of events, she was now inside a black SUV, going God-knows-where. Was this her life now?

"It'll be fine, don't worry," Daniel said as he sat beside her—now fully clothed—in the back seat of one the SUVs. The driver concentrated on the road, paying them no mind.

His calm voice soothed her like a balm. But that logical part in her brain told her that none of this was normal. "How do you know?"

"Jason's a good guy," he said. "He won't let anything bad happen to us."

A tingle ran up her spine when he placed a hand on her knee and rubbed back and forth. He was looking straight ahead, so she wondered if he realized what he was doing. The fact made her heart beat faster. It felt so natural and made her want to cuddle up to him again and feel his comforting embrace.

She leaned against the window instead and closed her eyes. Why did Daniel have to be so attractive? And nice? And protective? And have a big—

Whoa girl, she told herself. *Get a hold of those hormones.* But it was hard to not think of his large—attributes. Everything about him was *huge*. And difficult to ignore.

He was naked after he shifted back. What was I supposed to do?

How about, not stare, a wry voice answered rhetorically.

"I think we're here," he said, taking his hand from her knee as the vehicle slowed down.

"And where is here?"

He craned his neck to look outside. "I think we're at the Lennox Corporation headquarters."

"Lennox? Like your friend? John?"

"Jason," he corrected. "But, yeah, his family owns it. Actually, they own most of the town and the mountains too. The Lennoxes are a family of dragon shifters."

"D-dragons?" she stammered. "Like that other guy?" God, she'd never forget the sight of a fifty-foot flying serpent.

"Not quite. I think they're a different ... species? Anyway, don't worry, I played football with Jason in high school. And their family protects everyone in Blackstone." He looked at her reassuringly, those silvery blue eyes searching her face. "Nothing bad will happen, I promise."

The door opened, and Jason Lennox's head popped in. "Follow me, guys," he said.

Daniel hopped out first, and he helped her out of the SUV. Glancing around, she saw they were in some kind of underground parking garage. Thoralf—who had ridden in the other SUV with Jason—was already waiting for them by the elevators.

"Why are we at your office?" Daniel asked Jason.

"I'll explain when we get to the fifteenth floor." Jason pressed his thumb to the plate where there should have been a call button. The door slid open, and they entered the car. A few seconds later, the doors opened up again.

"Welcome to the marketing and research department of Lennox Corp.," Jason said as he stepped out of the elevator and gestured for them to follow.

"The what?" Daniel asked.

"Come on, let's go to the conference room. Christina and Luke are already waiting for us."

Jason led them across the room, which looked like any ordinary corporate office. Though it was late, there was still a flurry of activity going on as people rushed around or sat at their desks, typing away or talking on the phone.

"Go ahead," Jason said as he opened the door to a glass conference room. Thoralf went in first, and she and Daniel followed behind him. "Please, take a seat." He gestured to empty chairs and the three of them sat down along one side. "My wife and brother should be—oh, here they are."

Jason moved aside to let two people in—one was a tall, hulking man dressed casually in a T-shirt and jeans, and the other was a woman in a white skirt suit, her blonde hair pulled up in an elegant French twist.

"Hello," the woman greeted as she sat opposite them. "I'm Christina Lennox." Her accent was crisp and posh, and her expression business-like, but not totally unfriendly.

The man took a seat beside her. "Luke Lennox." His keen, tawny gold eyes scrutinized them one by one, as if assessing them for danger. Sarah let out a breath she didn't realize she was holding when Luke's gaze passed over her, seemingly not viewing her as a threat. She wondered what animal he turned into. Something large, with teeth, if that predatory gaze was an indication. Dear God, she'd never been around so many shifters before. It was unnerving.

Jason took a seat on the other side of Christina. "Christina, Luke, you guys know Daniel. But this is Thoralf, one of Aleksei's guards from the Northern Isles, and Sarah, Daniel's wife."

The word made her stomach flip, and she told herself it was because she wasn't used to the word yet. However, she made no move to correct him.

"You're probably wondering what this place is," Christina began. "Let me give you a rundown. Daniel, do you remember when that anti-shifter organization attacked the town last year?"

He nodded. "Yeah, of course. Anders and I found one of those explosives in sector 5-G."

"Explosives?" Sarah exclaimed, turning to Daniel. "There were explosives?" *And he had found them.* Panic crept into her gut thinking about what could have happened. What if it had exploded while he was around it? Or if he didn't find it and—

"Yeah. Don't worry, baby doll." He placed a soothing hand over her knee again. "PD was able to disarm them all. And our side won."

"Not quite," Jason said. "I mean, we stopped them from blowing Blackstone up that day, but it turns out, they're part of a much bigger problem."

"The people who tried to destroy Blackstone are part of an anti-shifter network called The Organization," Christina continued. "But they, in turn, are part of an even bigger and older circle called The Knights of Aristaeum."

"The Knights attacked my country," Thoralf said. "And they eliminated my king's—former king, that is—dragon."

"Eliminated?" Daniel's head swung toward the dragon. "What do you mean?"

"They had an artifact called The Wand that separates a shifter from his animal." Thoralf's expression hardened. "I'm ashamed to say that King Harald was under my protection when he was attacked and his dragon ripped away. Which is why I resigned my position as captain of the guard, and I'm now on a personal quest to restore the former king's dragon." He sighed. "I've been traveling all over the world for months now, and I have yet to find a solution. We have text and research that indicates there is a way to reverse The Wand's effects, but each clue so far has turned up a dead end or another clue. However, as I go along my quest, I have made it a point to pursue and thwart The Knights any way I can. Which is what brought me to Blackstone."

"What did you find out?" Luke asked.

"According to my sources, The Knights were coming here to Blackstone," Thoralf said. "And sending one of their top leaders, Lord Nox, to finish something that was left undone."

Daniel tensed. "I think I know what that something was."

"What?" Jason asked.

"Baker." His jaw hardened. "That white-haired guy said they came for me because I stopped that assassin from killing the VP."

Christina, Luke, and Jason all looked at each other, their expressions similar, as if something in their minds clicked together.

"What's going on?" Daniel said. "I mean, what's *really* going on? And you still haven't told us what this place is."

Christina pursed her lips and then folded her hands on top of the table. "You're at the headquarters of the Blackstone branch of The Shifter Protection Agency."

"Christina's father created The Agency to stop threats to our kind," Jason added. "And also, more recently, to advance our causes."

"What I'm about to tell you doesn't leave the room, okay?" Christina said. Everyone nodded. "Scott Baker wasn't just in Blackstone for a speech. It was a cover for a meeting here."

"Baker wants to help us," Jason continued. "Though he can't say it publicly because he'd lose the support of his party, he's very much pro-shifter. He might make a run in the next elections."

"A president that's openly pro-shifter?" Sarah exclaimed. "That's unprecedented." With Darcey being a shifter, she tried to keep up with all things shifter relations and politics. She wanted to be in the know in case anyone ever tried to hurt her sister.

Christina raised a brow at her. "True. But more than that, Baker's a good guy. Hates the prejudice that shifters experience and just wants to make the world a better place. We were going to meet about how he could assist in dismantling anti-shifter groups and put in more protections for shifters. The Organization and The Knights must have figured it out and tried to stop him."

"Their attempts were foiled by our friend here," Thoralf said, gesturing to Daniel.

"I'm sorry you were dragged into this mess." Jason shook his head. "Your wife, too."

It took a moment for the meaning of the words to sink in. "Me?"

"You guys are a target now," Luke said. "Believe me, those bastards won't stop until they get what they want. Or until you get to them first."

"What do we need to do, then?" Daniel said.

"We'll put a protective detail on you," Christina said. "Outfit you both with panic buttons and tracking devices."

"But how do we get to them?" Daniel's hands curled into fists. "Before they get to us? Where are they hiding?"

"Whoa, man." Jason held a hand up. "Calm down."

"Calm down?" Daniel grit his teeth. "They nearly killed my ma—wife! I'm going to find all of them and tear them to pieces."

Sarah stared at him, her jaw dropping to the ground. *Why was he acting weird?* Maybe it was the near-death experience that got him all riled up. And he was a good, selfless person after all. Surely his concern wasn't for her in particular, no matter how her heart thumped excitedly at the thought.

"We'll find them," Christina said confidently. "We have our guys working on it. Top priority."

"I should not have let them get away," Thoralf said with a shake of his head. "I was worried for Daniel and Sarah and decided to check on them first. And now The Knights will come back for them both because I failed once again." Turning to Daniel, he said, "I will protect you and your lady, Daniel Rogers. I swear, I will not leave your side until those who mean you and yours harm have been defeated."

"I suggest you stay home, Sarah," Christina said. "As much as you can. But Daniel is their target, and I don't think they'll come after you, especially since you're human. That's not their style."

"Stay home?" she asked. "As in *here*? In Blackstone?"

"Yes." The other woman's gaze narrowed. "Is that a problem?"

"But I don't live here," she said. "I need to go back to Las Vegas in a couple of days."

"Vegas?" Jason asked, then turned to Daniel. "But I thought you guys are married?"

"We are," he said.

"No, we're not." She let out a sigh as every single person there except for her and Daniel looked confused. "Oh God, this is so embarrassing, but here goes." She gave them the briefest version of what happened during that night in Las Vegas. "... and in a couple of weeks, when things die down, I'm going to file the annulment," she finished.

"I see," Christina said. "Knowing what you know tonight, do you still want to pretend you're staying married?"

"Yes," Daniel said.

"No," she said at the same time. "Wait, what do you mean?"

"We had an agreement," Daniel said. "And besides, The Knights already know who you are. The safest thing for you to do is stay here. Where I—The Agency can protect you."

"But Christina said they won't go after me."

"I said I don't *think* they'll come after you," Christina said. "But I can't predict what they'll do if they keep failing to get to Daniel."

"They can use her to get to me, right?" Daniel asked.

"Possibly, if they get desperate," Luke said.

"All the more reason for me to leave." This was crazy. All she wanted to do was get an annulment so she could get her bank loan, and now she was in the middle of some kind of shifter war. "I have a brother and sister back home. They need me."

"And you'll be leading The Knights back to them," Daniel pointed out. "Can't you see? Staying here is the safest option. Back in Vegas, you'd be vulnerable with no one to protect you."

"The Knights' reach is far and wide, my lady," Thoralf said. "If their eyes are fixed on you—and that is possible after tonight—they will pursue you."

She looked pleadingly at Christina, as she looked to be in charge. "Isn't there any other way? Witness protection or something?"

"There are places where we can hide you," she said. "But that still won't get you back to Vegas. But I can offer your brother and sister protection as well. I can have two agents watch out for them."

Sarah tapped her finger on her chin as she contemplated her choices. "I—fine." She took a deep breath.

"Good," Daniel said with a determined nod of his head. "You'll move in with me tonight."

Her head snapped to him. "What? Move in with you? We agreed I'd stay at the motel."

"That was before those bastards tried to kill you."

"They tried to kill *you*," she countered. "Not me."

"But they tried to take you too," he pointed out. "You heard Christina. You'll be safer at home. Mine."

"This is ridiculous, I can't stay with you."

"Yes, you can." He turned to Jason. "Dad put the house under an LLC before they left it to me. That should at least delay anyone digging through public records."

"Your dad's always been a smart one," Jason said.

"It would also sell your 'marriage' story better," Christina interjected.

"If you need to craft a statement, I'll have Lennox's PR

department do it for you," Jason offered. "They'll have something done by noon tomorrow and sent out once you approve it."

Sarah wanted to protest some more, but could see she was outnumbered. "Fine." An idea, however, popped into her head. "But, Thoralf should come too."

"Thoralf?" Daniel said, his voice edgy. "What do you want him for?"

"Well, I need someone to protect me, and he said he'll do it," she pointed out. "What are you going to do while you're working? Drag me up and down that mountain with you? And you said your house was huge. You won't even know he and I are there."

"Your lady has an excellent point, Daniel Rogers," Thoralf said. "Of course, if I am not welcome in your home, I understand. I would be happy to sleep outside."

"Sleep outside?" Sarah placed a hand on her chest. "Seriously, Daniel? This man saved your—our lives, and you're going to let him sleep on the ground when you have five perfectly good bedrooms in your gigantic home?"

"It's no trouble at all, my lady," Thoralf assured her. "I have slept in worse conditions in the last year. Why most of the time, I lay my head on whatever ground, tree, or cave I happen to be near."

"He hasn't even slept in a real bed in a while." She looked up at Daniel. "Please?"

Daniel ground his teeth loudly. "Fine," he relented. "He can stay with us."

"That should make our lives easier," Christina said. "Now, if you don't mind, maybe you guys can give us more details about the events of tonight, and give us any descriptions and details that might help us track down the men who attacked you."

Sarah leaned back in her chair and folded her arms over her chest. At least she wasn't going to be alone playing house with Daniel Rogers for the next few days.

It wasn't that she didn't want to live in his house. Oh God, there was a part of her that wanted it *too* much. This whole charade was bad enough, but something so intimate ... so close to him ... something told her it was a bad idea and would not end well. Dreaming of such things would only lead to disappointment.

Chapter 7

Jason, Christina, and Luke each talked to them separately. Sarah was glad it was Christina who interviewed her as she didn't feel comfortable with either of the men. Besides, she found herself admiring the other woman. She was obviously the one in charge around here, being a female surrounded by males at work—and the boss, to boot—was probably not easy.

After having their phones outfitted with a tracking app and panic button, they were finally free to go. Since Daniel's truck was trashed, The Agency lent him one of their SUVs and also promised to get her car back to her by morning. Soon, she, Daniel, and Thoralf were on their way. Before they left, however, they came up with a cover story that Thoralf was an old college buddy of Daniel's, who had done a year abroad in America and was visiting them for a couple of days.

Their destination wasn't too far, and the SUV slowed down as they reached a typical suburban street. It was dark but when she looked out the window, she saw that they'd pulled into the driveway of a sprawling Colonial-style home with its typical shuttered windows, pitched roof, and wooden clapboard siding.

"Wow." She couldn't help but gape. "It's beautiful."

"Thanks." Daniel stopped the truck and cut the engine.

What was it like to grow up in a home like this? Her own childhood hadn't been so idyllic mostly bouncing around a bunch of orphanages and foster homes. She was a difficult kid, on purpose most of the time, and the only reason she stuck around the last home was because of Darcey and Adam. Enduring that crappy living situation had been worth it, knowing that the moment she turned eighteen, she could take her brother and sister far away from that hellhole.

"It is indeed a splendid home," Thoralf exclaimed. "I'm honored you invited me to stay."

Daniel grunted but said nothing as he got out of the car, and they followed him toward the house. She nearly stumbled as she realized there was a ramp leading up to the front door instead of steps. Probably to make it easier to move furniture and other construction materials, she guessed.

Fishing the key from his pocket, he slipped it into lock. "I'm still finishing up the renovations."

"What was wrong with it?" she asked.

"Nothing, structurally." He pushed the door open. "But everything inside was outdated. I refinished the flooring, added some more modern lighting and appliances, ripped out the old wallpaper and repainted, bought new furniture, and installed an energy-saving boiler. Here we go."

They stepped into the entryway and followed him into the spacious living room. She had to bite her tongue to keep from saying *wow* again. Although the furniture was still covered in drop cloth and plastic tarps, it was obvious everything was done with love and care. The hardwood floors were polished to a shine, the paint cheerful and welcoming, and the lights illuminating the high ceilings creating a cozy atmosphere.

"I'm afraid I don't have sheets or towels down in the guest rooms, but I'll grab some from the linen closets. The kitchen has all the appliances and stuff, but I don't have it stocked with food. Do you need to go back to your motel and get some clothes?"

"I can manage for now," she said. "I'm honestly just exhausted. I can grab my things when I check out of the motel tomorrow."

"Sure," he said. "Now for the bedrooms. We have two upstairs and three down here."

"I think the safest strategy would be for me to bed down here," Thoralf suggested. "And you and Sarah stay upstairs."

"Sounds like a good plan." He nodded to the hallway on the left. "All the bedrooms down here have direct access to the garden and pool via a glass door."

"It will give me an opportunity to assess threats from the rear." He gave them a nod. "If you don't mind, I would like to perform a perimeter patrol for the next few hours."

"Patrol?" Sarah asked. "Aren't you tired?"

"I do not need much sleep or rest," he said. "Besides, we should always be on alert in case The Knights come back. Do not worry, I shall be quiet and not disturb you. I shall remain Cloaked as well. Goodnight." With a last bow, he headed down the hallway.

"Interesting fellow," she said wryly. "He's like a knight from King Arthur's time."

Daniel snorted. "Let's go upstairs, and I can show you your bedroom."

She followed him as he led her to the second floor, then headed inside the last door on the left. The bedroom was huge and had a king-sized bed in the middle, along with matching furniture done in dark woods. The bed itself was made with covers and decorative pillows, though there weren't any personal items anywhere. In fact, most of the house lacked any pictures or paintings, though she suspected that was because Daniel hadn't had time to put them back up.

"The walk-in closet over there is where I store the towels and stuff. The bathroom's next to it and the two rooms connect. Let me get my stuff, and I can be out of your way."

"Your stuff? This is *your* bedroom?"

"Kinda," he said, rubbing the back of his neck. "I mean, I still have my apartment, but this is where I sleep on the weekends when I'm out here fixing stuff. It used to be my childhood bedroom, but I expanded and updated it first since I knew I might crash here sometimes."

"But I can't stay here." It felt oddly intimate knowing Daniel had grown up here, slept here. And slept in *that* bed. "You should give me the other bedroom."

"That one faces the street," he said. "Besides, it's not finished. There's only a mattress in there and the shower's not done yet. You'd have to go downstairs to shower and stuff."

"But I can't take your bed," she sputtered. "I mean, I'm your guest. I shouldn't—"

"Just stay, okay?" Daniel grumbled, running his hands through his hair. "I'm tired, and it's been a long day. And, damn it, I don't wanna argue with you anymore."

His curt words made her shut her mouth. It was the first time Daniel had been anything less than polite to her. "Fine," she said, her tone chilly.

He must have noticed, because his expression changed. "I didn't mean to—"

"I'll stay out of your way," she said, brushing past him. "Good night." Striding into the bathroom, she shut the door behind her, then leaned back on it. She didn't move for a few seconds, not until she heard feet shuffling and the bedroom door closing.

God, she was tired, too. Could nothing just go her way, for once? All she wanted was one signature. That was all she'd came here for.

With a deep sigh, she walked over to the sink and washed her face. The bathroom was spacious and modern, and the deep tub in the corner looked tempting. But there was no time for that. For one thing, she still had to check in with Darcey and figure out what to do.

After doing her business, she stripped down to her underwear, took her phone out of her pants pocket and placed it on the bedside table before slipping between the covers.

"Oohhh," she moaned. *These sheets are divine.* And the mattress, too, was like sleeping on a cloud. Then there was that lingering, masculine scent all around her. A scent she was now familiar with. She'd probably wake up with it clinging to her naked body, a thought that made her shiver and her core clench. It would be so easy to just slip her hand down between her thighs and—

"Nuh-uh." She sat up, smoothing the covers down tightly around her waist. *Have to think of something else. Do something else.* Reaching for her phone, she checked her messages. There were several from her friends, but not really having the energy to explain it all, she sent them all the same apologetic message, promising to tell them everything as soon as possible. Then, she looked at the messages from Darcey. Her sister sent a couple of texts updating her on the orders for the day, but didn't seem freaked out that she hadn't replied. Thinking of another message to type sounded exhausting, so instead, she tapped on the green call button.

"Hey, Sarah," Darcey said when she picked up. "Did you get my messages?"

"Yeah, thanks for taking care of those things," she said. "How's Adam?"

There were a few seconds of silence, then Darcey blew out a breath. "I picked him up today, and it was obvious he found out while he was in school."

"He wasn't happy about it, I suppose." It was a statement, not a question.

"No," Darcey said. "He wouldn't even talk to me. Just locked himself in his room when we got home. But, don't worry, I'll talk to him, okay? We'll sort it all out when you come home. When are you back?"

She bit her lip. It was probably safer if Darcey didn't know about the whole attempt on her life thing. "In a few days. So, everything's okay with the site?"

"Yeah. That package went out just in time, and the lady at the Ship N' Click said you'll get it tomorrow first thing. So," Darcey began. "How are things with the hubs?"

"Ha. Were you waiting all day to ask me that?"

"Of course. It's not every day you find out you're married to a national hero. Is he even better looking in person?"

She let out a long, overdrawn yawn. "Woo, it's really late out here. I should get to bed."

Darcey giggled. "Oh, is that how it is? Fine. But you'll give me some real details when you get home, right?"

Home. A pang of loneliness hit her. Las Vegas and their crappy two-bedroom apartment seemed really far away right now. "I will. 'Night, Darce."

"'Night, Sarah." It was the way she, Darcey, and Adam always said goodnight to each other, ever since those days back in their foster home. When they turned off the lights in that tiny bedroom they shared, they could pretend everything was okay and they were the perfect family.

Another pang of loneliness hit her, and as soon as Darcey hung up, she sent out a text to Adam.

Can we talk? Just say the word and I'll drop what I'm doing to call you. Send. Her gaze remained on the screen as the seconds ticked by, but there weren't even any bubbles popping up on the chat to indicated he was typing.

"Fine." Putting the phone on the bedside, she sank back into the pillows. *Stubborn kid.* But she couldn't fault him for being, well, what he was—a teenager still trying to find his place in the world. When she took on the responsibility for raising Adam, she hadn't been much older than him, and there was no time for normal teen stuff. But she vowed to let Adam have the space he needed to have a normal childhood and figure out who he was. *Be careful what you ask for.*

The fake yawn seemed to have affected her more than she realized as she drifted off to sleep as soon as she closed her eyes. When she opened them again, it seemed like only a moment had passed, but light was already peeking through the gaps between the shades. Immediately, she reached for her phone, but still no reply from Adam. With a grumpy sigh, she went to the bathroom to wash up, got dressed, and headed downstairs.

"Good morning, my lady," Thoralf greeted cheerfully as she entered the kitchen. "An employee from The Agency has brought your vehicle back, and your keys are on the table by the door. He also informed me that Mrs. Lennox herself checked you out of your motel, and your things are in the trunk. Also, Daniel has brought us food and supplies."

The countertops in the bright, cheery kitchen were covered with various paper bags overflowing with boxes of food, veggies, and other household sundries.

"Awesome." Glancing around her, she wondered where Daniel was.

"Daniel has gone to work," Thoralf offered, as if reading her mind. "He informed me that he will be back later tonight, but to call him should we need anything."

Disappointment flooded her, but she ignored it. "All right. Have you eaten?"

His dark blond brows snapped together. "I confess I have not. My skills in the kitchen are quite limited, but I'm sure I can find some fruits or vegetables to eat." He dug through the bags and took out a bag of apples. "Ah! Something nutritious. This shall do."

She looked at him skeptically. "Surely you need more than that. Hold on." Searching through the first bag within her reach, she found some eggs, milk, and bread. "Ah, here we go. Why don't I make us some breakfast?"

"You don't need to—"

"It's fine, really. I'm starving."

It didn't take her too long to find everything she needed to put together a simple breakfast. Thoralf was happy to help root around the kitchen for things she needed or with tasks like breaking the eggs into a bowl or making toast. Soon, they were sitting down to some scrambled eggs, toast, juice, and coffee.

"This is most kind of you, my lady," Thoralf said as he took a spoonful of eggs into his mouth. "Delicious."

"Thanks. And please, call me Sarah." She didn't quite know what to make of the dragon shifter. It was almost like he stepped out of a medieval TV show or novel from the way he acted, talked, and dressed. This morning, he wasn't wearing his armor, but instead, donned a long-sleeved white shirt and tan pants. "So ... you've been traveling for a while now, Thoralf?"

"Yes." He took a gulp of orange juice. "My quest has taken me far and wide. I began in Europe and made my way through Asia, South America, and now I am here in the United States. It's my first time here."

"And you said you're from the Northern Isles?" she asked. "I'm afraid I've never heard of that country."

"Few have my—I mean, Sarah," he corrected. "We are a small country and prefer to be left alone. It's better that way to protect our people and natural resources. It's also a difficult place to get to unless one has a private plane or can fly on one's own."

"Like you?" Curiosity got the better of her. "You're a dragon, right?"

"A water dragon, yes." He took a large bite out of a piece of toast.

"Water dragon? There's more than one kind?"

"Yes, several in fact. My kind is different from the Blackstone dragons, who are mountain dragons. They are perhaps what you imagine when you think of dragons—large wings, sharp claws, and they breathe fire. Our queen, Queen Sybil, is one of them and is sister to Jason, Matthew, and Luke Lennox."

"Huh. I did remember something in the news last year about an American marrying some king of a small European nation. Do you miss home?"

A nostalgic look passed across his face. "Yes, I do, terribly. But I must complete my quest before I set foot on the Isles again. I must restore my lord's dragon." Pushing his empty plate away, he stood up from the kitchen counter stool. "Again, I thank you for this meal. I would be happy to clean up the dirty dishes as my share of the labor."

Hopping off the stool, she laughed. "I hate doing dishes, so yes, please. I'm going out to the car to get my stuff now."

She was grateful Christina thought to check her out and send her things—along with the overnight package from Darcey—saving her a trip back to the motel. Then she went in search of the laundry room to wash her dirty clothes and changed into fresh underwear and one of the dresses Darcey had sent.

As she did that, she checked her phone—still no reply from Adam—and her email and social media accounts for SLW. There were a number of interview requests from media outlets, but she ignored those. Surprisingly, she found a few nice messages from people who had discovered her website and well wishes on her marriage to Daniel.

There were also some *not-so-nice* ones. Though she was used to getting one or two pieces of hate mail from crazy people, she'd never received anything like this, specifically, those that called her a "shifter lover," "human traitor," and a bunch of other vile and disgusting names. *It was a good thing Darcey didn't have access to these accounts.* Though she was tempted to reply to all of them and give them a piece of her mind, it wasn't worth the trouble and brain cells, so all those messages were trashed and their senders blocked.

Feeling hungry sometime around one o'clock, she headed back to the kitchen and made herself a tuna sandwich. Thoralf was nowhere to be found, but she made him a couple of sandwiches in case he was hungry. There were more emails to answer, from her accountant, from the bank, and a few more orders and customer inquiries had come in. With all the busywork done, she could now get down to photographing the samples and put them up on the website.

With no extra cash to hire models, photographers, or even a website designer, Sarah did everything herself, learning how to use all the apps and programs to take and edit photos and put them up on the site. She modeled the lingerie pieces, used her phone and a tripod to photograph herself—from the neck down, of course—and a nifty app on her tablet to erase her tattoos so no one knew it was her. *Thank God for photo editing apps.* The last thing she needed was pictures of her in lingerie splashed all over the news.

Now, where to take the photos? Usually she used the white wall of the bedroom she shared with Darcey. There were a couple of white walls downstairs, but Thoralf might walk in on her. She didn't even want to think about having to explain that to him. *The bathroom!* Yes, the shower stall was huge, and the wall should work. The white tiles would be easy enough to erase.

After setting up her tripod and tablet in the bathroom, she selected her favorite among the samples—a red sheer lace teddy embroidered with roses and a T-strap choker. There were also matching garters and stockings which completed the look. She took a few test shots to adjust the settings and the positioning of the camera before she proceeded.

Modeling her creations was her least favorite part of the process, and she vowed that once she could afford it, she'd hire professionals to do this part. It took a long time because she had to take hundreds of shots before she could narrow it all down to about half a dozen or so that would be featured on each product page. As the timer on her tablet clicked away, she bent back with her hip cocked, stretching out her torso to elongate her body and show off the design.

"Sarah? Are you in here?"

The familiar masculine voice sent a jolt through her, which was unfortunate timing giving her current position. She yelped out as she started falling back, so she extended her arm. Grasping for anything that could prevent her fall, her fingers gripped the tap and twisted it, and a cold blast of water burst from the shower head.

"Motherfucker!" She steadied herself before she did fall, but the water continued to spray at her, blinding her. Her hands found the tap, thankfully, and turned it off. "Damn it!" She was soaking wet. "Goddamm—oh shit."

The door had burst open, and Daniel careened into the bathroom. "Sarah! Are you hurt? Is—" He stopped short, his jaw dropping as his eyes landed on the camera set up—and her.

Kill me now. "I can explain." Warmth crept up her ... well, everywhere. "T-this isn't what you think it is." *Oh God, I'm in trouble.* Daniel probably thought she was a cam girl or worse, that she was using his home to turn her tricks.

A spark of something lit up his silvery blue eyes. Something she didn't want to name. "Oh yeah?" He took a few steps closer. "Do you want to know what I think this is?"

The low thrum of his voice caressed over her skin like a lover's touch, and her mouth went dry as a desert. She was in deep trouble, but not in the way she thought she was.

Chapter 8

After last night's debacle, Daniel knew staying away from Sarah for now would be the best thing. He'd been curt to her, and he hated that those were the last words she heard from him, but he didn't know what to do. It had been a long, tiring day, and arguing with her only agitated his grizzly even more. His animal didn't know why their mate was being belligerent when they only wanted to protect her and why she didn't want to stay in their den. But he couldn't make it understand, and when he told it that he didn't want to argue anymore, he had inadvertently said it out loud, and Sarah thought he had said it to her. He wanted to explain, but it was obvious she wasn't hearing any of it.

So, he went to bed, got up early to grab some groceries, and left for work. He stayed inside the office, only because he didn't want to have to face anyone else, though all he wanted to do was go back home and see Sarah again.

His grizzly snarled at the thought of her alone with that other male. His human side knew that the dragon shifter had no interest in Sarah, but all his shifter side saw was a rival for their mate's affections. No amount of explaining or pleading could convince the bear otherwise.

Finally, it was time to clock out, and he drove home. Thoralf was nowhere in sight, but he had the distinct feeling that the dragon shifter was somewhere around. Probably using his creepy-ass ability to Cloak himself so he could lurk around the perimeter unseen.

Seeing as Sarah wasn't downstairs, he went up to the bedroom, intending to apologize. She didn't answer when he knocked or even when he called her, so when he heard her shout, his protective instincts went into overdrive and he burst in. His imagination ran wild. Did The Knights find them? Were they holding her in there? Or was Thoralf in there with her, and it was a different kind of scream? His grizzly was ready to burst out of his skin at that point to tear any rival off her.

But this ... this wasn't what he was expecting.

Jesus Almighty.

She had that deer in headlights look as she stood in the shower stall, dripping wet and dressed in that sinful red concoction. "T-this isn't what you think it is."

Daniel knew what he should do. He should act like a gentleman, back away, and close the door to give her some privacy. It's what he'd been taught all his life, the principles he lived by. *Wait. Be patient. Ask, don't just take.*

But he was tired of that. Of being *the nice guy.* He wanted to take, to claim. He wanted *Sarah.* "Oh yeah?" He moved a few steps closer. "Do you want to know what I think this is?"

Her plush lips parted, and her gaze lowered, her sweeping lashes leaving shadows over her dusky cheekbones. *Fuck.* Seeing her like this ... dressed in nothing but red lace ... She trembled as he stepped into the shower. "Sarah." Reaching out, he touched his finger to her chin and tipped her head up. "Sarah," he repeated.

Her lids opened, those soft brown eyes looking up at him with unmistakable desire. His finger traced a trail down her chin, to her throat, his entire hand covering the bit of lace around her neck in a gentle, but possessive grip. Her pupils blew out, and the scent of her arousal teased his nostrils.

Fuck it.

He slammed up against her, pressing her body up the tiled wall as his mouth slotted over hers. His blood sang in his veins, and he knew this was not the first time their lips had met. She didn't hesitate in responding either, as she opened her mouth to him and slid her hands up to his shoulders to pull him closer.

Slipping his tongue into her mouth, he tasted her sweetness. Bits of memories flooded his brain telling him he knew this taste and this body pressed up against him. That didn't make him want her less, in fact, he craved more of her. He devoured her mouth, and she eagerly let him, giving him more, her lips and tongue tasting and battling his. *Feisty.* He groaned at her eagerness, wanting more. And he would take it.

His hands planted at her hips, sliding up her lace-covered ribcage to cup her breasts. This, too, seemed familiar, the weight of her breasts in his hands. Pulling away from her, he licked and kissed a path down her neck.

"Daniel." Her warm husky voice laced with longing went straight to his cock. Now fully hard, it strained painfully against his pants. Squeezing her breasts together, he licked at her cleavage, eliciting a moan from her. His thumbs found her nipples through the wet lace, and he covered one with his mouth.

Fingers raked through his hair and gripped the roots. That only made him groan against her breast and suckle the stiff nipple through the lace harder. Her hips start to roll against him, and he knew what she wanted.

Moving even lower, he kneeled in front of her. He saw the

snaps holding the teddy between her legs, and he pulled them apart. "Ffuucck." Her pussy was pink, shaved, and absolutely perfect like everything about her. Lifting one knee up, he hoisted it over his shoulder. The smell of her was powerful, and his cock twitched painfully, but he was determined to give her pleasure first, so he teased her by licking around her thighs.

"Daniel," she panted. "Please."

The word coming from her mouth broke something in him, and he pressed his mouth to her clit. She gasped and clutched at his hair harder, her hips pushing up. He lapped her little bud with quick, hard strokes that had her panting.

"Keep going. Oh God!"

He could feel her at the edge of her orgasm as he continued to lap at her. However, just as she was about to come, he slowed down. She let out a frustrated grunt, and he couldn't help but smile.

Spreading her thighs more, he slipped a finger in her, making her yelp out. He stroked her deep, making a "come here" sign with his finger, and she grew wetter with each stroke. Looking up, he saw her eyes roll back as she squeezed hard around him. Knowing she was close, he put a second finger inside and then slid his tongue across her clit.

"Daniel! *Ohfuckohfuckohfuck*!"

Her pussy gripped his fingers tight as her entire body went rigid. Her hips bucked against his mouth as she flooded him with her slickness, a litany of curses spewing from her mouth as she came. He continued to pump her with his fingers even as she shuddered and her body went limp.

"God, Sarah," he groaned. "I need you so bad."

Her breath came in deep gulps. "Yes. Daniel ..."

He hauled himself up and captured her lush mouth again, letting her taste herself. She kissed him eagerly, even as her hands went to the front of this uniform shirt to unbutton it. Reaching down, he unzipped his fly and pushed down his briefs, his cock springing out. He wrapped his hand around his shaft, and she spread her legs eagerly to accommodate him.

A loud crash jolted him out of his desire-fogged haze, and every hair on the back of his neck rose as lust was replaced with danger. He quickly pulled away from her.

Her eyes snapped open. "What the—"

"Stay here," he commanded, as he righted himself. "I heard something. There's trouble downstairs.'"

"W-what?" Her gaze was still clouded. "You're kidding, right?"

She didn't hear it, of course, because she wasn't a shifter. "Where's your phone?"

"I-in the bedroom."

"Use your panic button," he said before turning toward the door. "And lock yourself up here."

"But—"

Though it pained him to leave her, he knew she was safer here. Hopefully, the agency would send someone right away, but he would take care of whoever that intruder was. As he rushed out of the bedroom, he didn't hear any more crashes or commotions, but there was still noise coming from downstairs. It sounded like two people arguing.

"... I said I want to see her, *now*!"

Rage pushed him to use his shifter speed, and he reached the bottom of the stairs in half a second.

"Young man, if you would please calm down—"

"I am fucking calm! Get my sister or I'll—"

"What the hell is going on here?" This was not what he'd expected. Not at all.

Thoralf stood in the entryway to the living room, not

moving a muscle, while a man in a wheelchair faced him, one hand raised menacingly at the dragon shifter.

"I said, what's going on here?"

The wheelchair-bound man turned his head toward him. *Jeez, he's just a kid.* Probably fifteen or sixteen, with wheat-blond hair and green eyes. Eyes that widened in recognition when his gaze fixed on Daniel.

"*You,*" he said, swinging his hand around. "This is your fault."

"My fault?" Daniel saw something spark in the kid's hand. "Is that a taser?"

"Where's Sarah?" he asked.

"Sarah?" His body tensed, and his grizzly bared its teeth. "How do you know her? Who are you?"

"Daniel?" Footsteps pattered down the stairs. "Daniel, who's down—Adam?"

"I told you to stay upsta—hold on." His gaze ping-ponged from her to the teen in the chair. "You know this kid?"

Sarah, now dressed in a shirt and jeans, stopped halfway down the steps, blood slowly draining from her pretty face. "He's my brother. What are you doing here, Adam? How did you get all the way here?" Rushing down, she sailed toward the kid and knelt to his level. "Does Darcey know you're here? She must be out of her mind with worry! And how did you get here anyway?"

"You said you wanted to talk," Adam sneered. "Well, here I am. Were you even going to tell me about him?" He glared at Daniel. "They said you were married three months ago. Why would you keep something like that from me?"

She turned even paler. "I didn't ... I mean, I wasn't—"

"I had to find out from those assholes at school." His face turned red as he clenched his fists. "And they found your website, too. Don't even get me started about that. Did you have some secret life you weren't telling me about all this time? Were you going to run off with your new husband and your new business and leave me and Darcey behind? Is that why you didn't tell me?"

"No!" Her voice shook as she tried to put her hands over his, but he pushed them away. "P-please, Adam, it's not like that."

"What else could it be?"

"Adam, I can't explain right now," she sobbed. "I'm just ... it's not what you think. I would never leave you and Darcey behind."

"You said we would always be together. And that—that we were family." His voice cracked. "That was a lie, too, wasn't it?"

"Adam, no, please."

The tears streaking down Sarah's cheeks made Daniel's heart ache. "All right now," he began, then took a deep breath. "I think we're all tired and had a long day." How the heck did this kid get all the way here anyway? "Adam, why don't you give me your weapon?" The kid shot him a death glare and clutched the stun gun tighter. "All right. You can keep it. But you must be hungry. How about you get something to eat? Thoralf could you help us out?"

The dragon shifter nodded. "I have already begun heating up a 'frozen pizza.' I did not want to bother any of you, but I was already famished. I must admit, the settings on the oven intimidated me, but the instructions on the box were quite thorough. Do you think you could check if I have done this correctly, young man?"

Adam gave him a look that said, 'are you for real?', but when Thoralf didn't flinch, he nodded. "Fine." Placing the taser on his lap, he wheeled himself forward, following behind Thoralf.

Sarah stood there, frozen as she stared after her brother. "You probably have questions," she finally said when Adam disappeared into the kitchen.

"You don't have to explain anything," he said. Tentatively, he reached out to touch her shoulder. She didn't flinch, but instead, leaned into his touch. "But do you want to talk about it?"

Turning to him, she wiped her cheeks with the back of her hand. "Adam isn't my biological brother. But he, our sister Darcey, and I were at the same foster home for a time. I was fourteen, Darcey, thirteen, and Adam was seven. He'd already been in a wheelchair then, because his biological dad beat him up so bad, it injured his spine permanently. His mother couldn't care for him, so she left him with the state."

A surge of rage tore through Daniel and his grizzly. What kind of monsters would do that to their own child? "I didn't realize you were raised in a foster home."

"Several, actually. My parents abandoned me when I was four." When he opened his mouth, she shook her head. "No, I don't know who they are, and I don't remember. I think ... they might have been migrant farmers working in California. CPS found me wandering around the road somewhere in Bakersfield. I only knew my name and my age."

"Sarah ..." Unable to stop himself, he pulled her into an embrace, not even giving her a chance to struggle. "I'm sorry," he murmured into her hair.

"It's fine. I got over it. They put me in an orphanage for a bit, then that's when I started bouncing around foster homes." She shrugged away from him, and though he didn't want to let her go, he did so anyway. "Then I was placed with Eddie and Josie McLaren. Those pieces of shit only used kids for the money. Darcey and Adam had already been there a couple of months when I arrived. It was ... horrible, to say the least. The house was always filthy, there wasn't always enough to eat, and the McLarens drank heavily and would scream at us for any little thing we did. Usually, I'd start acting out so my foster parents would have no choice but to call my case worker and take me away, but I couldn't do that to them. They were so helpless, Darcey and Adam. I couldn't leave them behind."

"So, you stayed."

"Yeah. Four more years. Worked every job I could, saved my money, and even managed to graduate high school. As soon as I turned eighteen, I took Darcey and Adam and ran away from that place. The McLarens didn't seem to care because they got their checks anyway, and CPS was too busy to check up on us. Just like dozens and dozens of kids in the system, Adam and Darcey just fell through the cracks."

"And you were there to catch them." He stared at her in complete awe. His mate was absolutely ... amazing. Selfless and beautiful, inside and out. If he wasn't in love with her already, he was mostly there.

She harrumphed. "You make it sound like I'm some kind of hero. But they're my family, you know?" Tears welled up in her eyes. "I'm doing my best for Adam. At least I thought I was. We've been fighting a lot and ... and now ... oh!" she cried. "He must think I'm doing the same thing his mom did. Abandoning him." She snapped her fingers. "I need to tell him that I'm not doing that. Reassure him that I'll never leave him."

"Wait," he said, catching her arm before she ran into the kitchen.

"But I have to go see him—"

"Just wait a sec, okay? Look." He paused to get his thoughts together. "I've been that age before. He's been through a rough time, probably got a lot of teasing and bullying because of his condition and his home situation. I can kind of relate."

She nodded. "But I can't imagine anyone bullying *you*."

"Believe me, teen boys will find anything to tease another kid about." He scratched his chin. "If you go in there and start mothering him, he'll just keep closing himself off. He needs time and rest. And so do you."

"But—"

"No buts. You need to step away for now. Why don't you call your sister and tell her what's going on? Like you said, she must be sick with worry."

"Darcey. Right."

"Meanwhile, after Adam's done eating, I'll get him settled into one of the bedrooms."

"I—wait." She stared at him, slack-jawed. "You're letting him stay?"

"Of course I am. I'm not tossing a kid out into the streets. He can stay as long as he needs to."

"I didn't say—I thought—" She pursed her lips. "Thank you. Thank you so much."

"Don't worry, okay? I'll take care of him." From now on, he wanted to take care of everything for her. "By the way, how the heck did he get all the way here from Las Vegas?"

She rolled her eyes. "Adam's kind of a genius. His IQ is off the charts and he loves computers. Last year he wanted to go to Burning Man to meet his Internet friends, but of course we wouldn't let him go. Somehow, he got on a bus to Reno, then found some other people on their way to the festival and caught a ride with them in their RV. He was halfway there by the time we caught up to him." She covered her eyes with her hand. "So I'm not at all surprised he got here so quick."

"Smart kid," he said. "Anyway, go tell your sister that he's fine. I'll check on Thoralf and Adam. I don't smell anything burning so at least I know they got the pizza figured out."

She opened her mouth and then closed it again. "Thank you." Turning on her heel, she sprinted back upstairs.

Daniel watched her go, then headed into the kitchen. Thoralf and Adam were already at the kitchen table.

"Ah, there he is. Daniel, come join us!" Thoralf waved him over and pointed to the extra-large pie on the table. "This pizza is delicious. And young Adam here was telling me about his journey. I must admit, he is quite crafty and cunning. Imagine, he was able to come here purely by his own wiles."

"Can I sit here?" he asked, nodding at the empty chair next to Adam.

Adam looked at him suspiciously, but shrugged. "It's your house."

Sitting on the chair, he helped himself to two slices of pizza. "Listen, Adam," he began. "I know you're probably angry at Sarah. And I get that." He took a bite, chewed, and swallowed. "Our family was so ... different, and the other kids at school teased me for it. I got mad a lot at my parents when I was your age. But my dad always said that words can be more powerful than any weapon. And when you say something, you can never, ever take it back, so you have to be careful how and when you use them."

Adam didn't say anything, but just kept eating his pizza.

"You don't have to talk to Sarah tonight. Or to any of us. In fact, I don't recommend it. Cool off, get a shower, have a good night's sleep. You'll feel better in the morning, I promise you that."

His head snapped up. "I can sleep here?"

"Of course. There's a room next to Thoralf's that you can use. I think you'll like it. You can open the glass door and sit out on the patio. We have a pool too, and you can swim in the morning if you want."

Adam polished off the last of his slice. "Okay."

"I have more food if you're hungry. How about juice? Or soda?" He nodded at the fridge. "They're in there, help yourself. Maybe you can grab some for us, too?"

Thoralf made a move to stand, but Daniel looked at him

meaningfully, so he relaxed. Adam wheeled himself toward the fridge, opened the door, and grabbed three cans of soda. "Thanks, man," he said, taking one of the cans the teen offered.

"How about I grab one of those beers too?" Adam asked slyly.

"Now you're pushing it, kid," Daniel retorted, but chuckled after, bringing a wide smile to the young man's face.

"Hey."

All three of them turned toward Sarah, who stood in the doorway. Adam then looked to Daniel. "I think I'd like to get cleaned up now."

He nodded. "Thoralf will show you the room."

The dragon shifter got to his feet. "Of course. Come with me, young man."

Sarah moved aside as Thoralf headed toward her, Adam rolling behind him. She looked distraught, but as Adam passed by her, he slowed down. "'Night, Sarah," he whispered.

"'Night, Adam," she called, her lower lip trembling as she watched her brother leave the kitchen.

"Are you all right?" Daniel asked when they were alone.

Her breath hitched, but she nodded. "Thank you."

"You're welcome. Have a seat. And a slice."

"I—No, it's okay. I'm not hungry."

"But—"

"Really, I'm exhausted. I just want to crawl into bed and sleep."

Daniel desperately wanted her to stay and sit with him, and more important—talk about what happened in the bathroom—but he could see she really was tired. Her body slumped forward like a deflated balloon. "All right, I'll clean up and leave the slices in the fridge in case you get hungry."

"Thanks." Pivoting on her heel, she shuffled out of the kitchen.

Once he heard her rush up the stairs and the door of the bedroom close, he let out a breath and buried his head in his hands. *This was going to be a long night*

The next day when he opened his eyes, Daniel immediately sat up so he could get ready for work, then remembered it was Saturday, his day off. He was hoping to have some time alone with Sarah today, but he guessed that wouldn't be happening, not with Thoralf and Adam around. He didn't resent the kid for coming here, but now that he understood their situation more, he knew that there were more important things. Yes, even more important than getting laid. Even more important than seeing Sarah in—and out of—that sinful outfit again.

God, his cock got so hard when he remembered what happened in the shower, it was almost painful. He supposed he could take care of himself, but it seemed weird, having all those people in the house, plus, it would only satisfy him temporarily. His body craved for the real thing.

After a very long, cold shower, he got dressed and bounded downstairs. He could smell bacon frying all the way from the hallway, so he followed his nose to the kitchen. The sight that greeted him made his heart leap out of his chest. Sarah was by the stove, her hair pulled up into a messy bun, wearing an apron over some kind of pajama top and shorts, humming to herself as she leaned over a frying pan. This was something he wanted to see every morning for the rest of his life—her, looking so relaxed and at home in his house. He watched her for a few more seconds before clearing his throat.

"Oh." She turned to him. "I hope you don't mind. I made breakfast." She nodded to the table that was already heaped with food—a pile of toast, a mountain of eggs, and a platter of bacon.

"Not at all, thank you for making it." He slid up next to her and leaned over, pretending he was looking into the pan, but really, he wanted a whiff of her scent. "Smells amazing."

"It's the last of the bacon," she said.

"How are you feeling?"

Her shoulders slumped. "I couldn't sleep," she confessed. "I just kept thinking about Adam. What I'm going to say to him." Turning off the flame, she wiped her hands on the apron and rubbed her temple. "He deserves the truth. He's old enough. I know he's ready to face ... these things."

"Then, what's the matter?"

"*I'm* not ready." She looked up at him sheepishly. "See ... I've been his mother figure for half of his life now. And I know he's always looked up to me. I'm not ready for him to see that I could do stuff like that. Get drunk and ... other things. I mean, I've dated before. Always discretely, and he's never met any of those men because I'd never been comfortable enough with any of them. But I can't show him that ... that ..."

"That you're a normal human being?" His tone turned serious. "That you're an adult woman with feelings and needs and wants."

That last word sparked something between them, and he knew she was thinking of what happened in the bathroom. He reached out toward her. "Sarah, I—"

"Good morning!" Thoralf's booming voice echoed across the kitchen, and Sarah whipped around and busied herself with the pan. "Another breakfast feast, I see." His eyes scanned the table laden with food. "I have never been so well fed and warmly welcomed anywhere." He stepped aside to let Adam roll in. "You are so lucky, Adam, to have a sister who cooks breakfast so skillfully."

Adam sniffed at the table. "I'm starving," he said to Sarah. "Can we eat now?"

"Of course." Sarah excitedly ran over to him. "Do you want some juice? Or some water? Coffee? Let me get some food for you."

The teen shifted uncomfortably. "I'm fine." He yanked the plate away before she could grab it. "I can feed myself, okay?"

She shrank back but nodded. "Okay. I'm here, just tell me what you need."

Her nervous energy made the atmosphere even more awkward. Daniel understood that she was edgy, but she was probably making things worse by coddling him, especially in front of two other males. But at the same time, he hated seeing his mate in distress like this. An idea popped into his head. "So, Adam, do you know anything about Blackstone?"

"Only that it's a town full of shifters." He bit into a strip of bacon. "You're a grizzly, right? What about you?" he asked Thoralf. "What are you?"

"Adam!" Sarah admonished. "That's rude."

"What?" he said through a mouthful of bacon. "I've only ever been around one shifter, and Darcey isn't anywhere near a bear or wolf or lion. I bet he's something *huge*."

Sarah's sister was a shifter? Now he was even more intrigued. But he filed that away for now. "Yes, that's true about Blackstone, and yes, I'm a grizzly bear. I'll let Thoralf answer your other question if he wants to. But, aside from that, Blackstone is also known for its mountains. There're tons of things to do up there if you like the outdoors. Camping, swimming in the lake, and lots of hiking trails that'll bring you up to some awesome views. Would you like to go up and see some with me today?"

The teen glared at him. "Are you stupid or somethin'?"

"Adam!" Sarah looked daggers at her brother. "This is

Daniel's home. Watch your mouth. God, what is it with you today?"

The teen's lips peeled back. "In case you haven't noticed, I'm never ever going hiking with these." He slapped a hand on his legs. "So, no, I don't want to go hiking with you, unless you wanna carry me all the way up there."

Sarah's face was all red now, and her breathing turned ragged. Reaching over, he placed a soothing hand over her knee. "The Blackstone Mountains is one of the most wheelchair-accessible forest reserves in the United States," he began. "There are several trails that are wheelchair-friendly."

Adam's eyes widened as he swallowed audibly. "Really?"

"Yeah. A local ADA advocate petitioned to have those trails built, and the rangers and the Lennox Foundation were only too happy to oblige." He couldn't help the smile that tugged up the corners of his mouth. "His mate, you see, loved hiking up in those mountains, and they wanted to share that together."

He seemed in awe at first, but in a very teen-like way, shrugged his shoulders. "I guess that would be nice."

Daniel fought another smile. "Sure. Maybe you and I could check it out first. Before we invite anyone to come." Sarah looked like she wanted to protest, but he squeezed her knee harder.

"Yeah, I can do that." Grabbing the plate of eggs, he heaped some onto his plate and shoveled it into his mouth.

The rest of the breakfast passed by in relative silence, though the tension had somewhat eased.

When every bit of food was gone, he said to Adam, "Go and get ready, and we'll leave in twenty minutes." Catching Sarah's eye, he cocked his head toward the doorway and then got up and strode out. Thankfully, he heard her chair scrape the tile as she stood up to follow him.

"You didn't have to do that," she said when they were in the hallway out of earshot. "It's your day off, isn't it? You shouldn't have to go into work today."

"It's no trouble at all," he said. "Really, I love being up there. Look, it's obvious to me that neither of you are ready to talk to each other yet. At least this way, I'm buying you time to think about what you have to say to him."

She bit her lip. "I think ... I think Adam always wished he could do stuff like this. You know, sports and outdoor things. He never gets to do it. There just wasn't any opportunity or time or money to get him all the special stuff he'd need." Her gaze dropped to the floor. "I wish—"

"Stop that."

Her head snapped up. "Stop what?"

"Beating yourself up for things that aren't your fault." Gently, he wrapped his hands around her arms. "Can't you see what an amazing job you've done raising a kid when you were one yourself? And what an incredible job you're still doing providing for his needs, and not just financially? Adam seems like a great kid despite all the challenges he's had to face. And you did that."

Her mouth dropped open, but nothing came out. All he could do was stare down at her lips as his heart beat madly in his chest. God, he wanted to just kiss her senseless right now. Right here in the hallway, then carry her up to his bed and finish what they'd started yesterday.

Someone clearing their throat, however, made him drop his hands to his sides. "Excuse me," Thoralf said. "I hate to interrupt."

"You're not interrupting." Sarah smoothed her hands down her front.

Annoyed, he turned to the other man. "What is it?"

"Will you be needing me to accompany you on your hike?"

he asked. "If you wish, I could fly overhead and remained Cloaked and out of sight."

"No, Adam and I will be fine."

"All right then, I shall stay here with Sarah."

"Actually," he began, "I have a better idea. Why don't you go out and do something? Explore the town. You can't stay in the house the whole day." While his grizzly was not fine with leaving Sarah with another male, Daniel knew Thoralf was trustworthy and would protect her. "Sarah? What do you think?'

"I don't know." She worried at her lip. "There's nothing I can think of that I want to do. I'm not much of a shopper, nor am I the type to sit and read at a cafe all day."

"What do you like to do to relax then?"

Her forehead wrinkled. "Sleep. And maybe do some yoga."

"You're in luck then," he said. "There's a new fitness studio in town, and I happen to know the owner."

"You do?"

"Yeah. The place is called Blackstone Bodyworx. Thoralf can go with you."

"I'll accompany her and make sure she is well protected," the dragon shifter said.

"Great, I'll give Anna Victoria a call now, and she'll book you into a class."

"What? No, you can't—"

On impulse, he kissed the tip of her nose. "Yes, I can." That seemed to stun her into silence. "I need to get ready, okay? So, go, have a relaxing day, and we can meet at Rosie's at seven." He didn't bother to wait for her to protest and left her in the hallway as he sprinted up the steps. A hike should help distract him, plus, it'll help him get to know Adam better and give Sarah some breathing room.

It was obvious she had very little time to spoil herself,

having to raise two siblings on her own the last couple of years. *That was going to change.* At least it would once they were mated and bonded. *Can't forget that.* With all the craziness of the last two days, he'd almost neglected his real focus. Winning her over would be tough seeing as they wouldn't have any alone time, but he was determined to keep Sarah and, fake marriage be damned, make her his, permanently.

Chapter 9

Sarah stared up at the neon-lit sign above the double glass doors that said "Blackstone Bodyworx." The studio's green and blue logo featured a stylized scribble of three human figures that formed the shape of a mountain range.

"This is the exercise studio Daniel recommended?" Thoralf said.

"Looks like it."

"Hmm." He rubbed his thumb and forefinger on his beard.

"What's wrong, Thoralf?"

"There are too many people around." Glancing around, his eyebrows furrowed together. "It is a challenge to assess the dangers and find an exit should things go wrong."

The Blackstone Bodyworx studio was located along a row of shops in the trendy shopping and entertainment district of South Blackstone. It was a busy Saturday afternoon, so the place was packed. Had she known it was going to be this crowded, she would have gone earlier instead of finishing up her work for the day and leaving later in the afternoon. But she had to finish photographing the new collection, editing the photos, and put them up on the website. By the time she was done, it was already past four o'clock in the afternoon.

"I'm sure it's fine," she said.

"Also, people are staring at us wherever we go. Perhaps they recognize you? I doubt The Knights would be so bold." Two women walked by them, their heads turned to rubberneck as they passed. Their eyes were so fixed on Thoralf that they didn't see the bench in their way, and one of them smacked into it, sending her tumbling over.

Sarah suppressed a laugh, doubting that she was the reason the two women were looking at them. At nearly seven feet in height, Thoralf demanded attention, but his broad shoulders, muscled chest, and handsome looks made him more than stand out. "I don't think it's me."

"I should have remained Cloaked." Thoralf had explained to her that dragons like him had the ability to turn invisible in both human and dragon form.

"I told you, that would be weird." And unnerving, too, as she imagined walking around town with an invisible protector looking over her shoulder. "Anyway, let's go inside, shall we?"

She pushed the door open and strode inside, Thoralf right behind her. The waiting area by the entrance was airy and well-lit. The exposed brick and air ducts gave it an industrial modern feel that went well with the rest of the building, but the cozy couches, plants, and stacks of fitness books and magazines gave it a welcoming atmosphere. On the other side of the room was a counter where two women stood, chatting in low voices. The one behind the counter wore athletic attire, her blonde hair pulled up in a sleek ponytail. The woman on the other side wore a loose shirt and shorts, her messy mop of flaxen hair half-hidden under a trucker hat.

"... I swear, I tried to get her to come," trucker hat said. "But I think she's still feeling guilty about letting you down."

Blondie sighed. "Really? The wedding was three months ago. And she didn't let me down, the ceremony was only delayed because of the dress. How did she look?"

Trucker hat shrugged. "The same. But she wouldn't even let me in, just peeked through the door."

"We should ask—" Blondie stopped when Sarah came closer. "Oh, hello. Welcome to Blackstone Bodyworx. How can I help you?"

"Uh, hi. Are you Anna Victoria? Daniel sent me."

Pansy-blue eyes widened. "Oh. Yes, I am. And you must be Daniel's Sarah."

Daniel's Sarah?

Trucker hat turned around. "You're *her*?" Her face lit up as she grabbed Sarah's hands and shook it vigorously. "I've read about, er, I mean, *Anna Victoria* told me all about you. I'm—" Her mouth gaped open as her gaze landed somewhere over Sarah's left shoulder, then lifted up. "I'm ... uh ..."

Sarah didn't need a second guess as to what she was looking at.

"J.D.," Anna Victoria said wryly. "Her name is J.D."

J.D.'s hazel eyes bugged out of their sockets. "Or whatever you want it to be."

Sarah burst out with a chuckle. "This is Thoralf." She gestured to the dragon shifter. "He's Daniel's friend from college, visiting from Sweden."

He acknowledged them with a nod. "Ladies."

"Close your mouth or you'll catch flies," Anna Victoria said to J.D. before turning to Sarah. "So, you're just in time for our last class of the day, which is in fifteen minutes." She took something from behind the counter and handed it to her. "Here," she said, a paper bag dangling from her fingers. "These should be your size, but if anything doesn't fit, just let me know, and I'll swap it out."

Frowning, she took the paper bag and peeked inside. There was what looked like a sports bra on top. "Oh, do you give all your students new stuff?"

"Oh no, not at all. But Daniel said you didn't have any exercise clothes, so he asked me to pick a couple of things for you. Aside from the bra, there's a pair of shorts, a towel, and a tank top in there."

"Thanks." Taking her wallet out of her purse, she opened it. "How much do I owe you?"

"What? No, no, Daniel paid for it. And the class, too."

"What? No, I can't let him do that. Here's a twenty—"

Anna Victoria pushed her hands and cash away. "I can't, sorry, it's all been paid for."

"I ..." She couldn't believe Daniel would pay for everything. "Thanks."

"Welcome. Locker room's over there, second door on the left. Will you be attending, too, Mr. Thoralf?"

"It's just Thoralf, my lady," he said. "I had not planned on it, but I must admit, I have never done any yoga and am intrigued. My muscles could use some stretching."

"I'll help you out," J.D. offered enthusiastically. "I'd love to stretch those muscles."

Anna Victoria rolled her eyes. "All right then," she said. "I still have some spots left. You can join us."

"I shall need proper attire as well." He produced a black credit card and placed it on the counter. "Please give me whatever you need."

"I'm gonna get dressed. See you in class."

Following Anna Victoria's directions, she found the locker room and got dressed in the new workout clothes. They fit well, surprisingly, and when she was done, she walked out into the main studio.

There were a few students milling about already, chatting or stretching out on the mats. She took a spot near the back next to J.D., who was sitting cross-legged on her mat. Before she could chat her up, Anna Victoria entered the studio, Thoralf behind her. Every single pair of female eyes riveted on him, and Sarah couldn't blame them. He was dressed in black cycling shorts and a matching tank top that showed off his rock-hard shoulders and tattooed arms. He didn't seem fazed however, as he met her gaze, waved, and then took the empty spot all the way in the back.

"Good afternoon, everyone," Anna Victoria greeted. "Welcome to our class. Let's start, shall we?"

Sarah turned her attention to Anna Victoria, listening to her instructions as she went through the flow. One of the things she loved about yoga was that for at least an hour, she could forget about the outside world and her worries and concentrate on her body movements. She'd gone to many yoga classes over the years, and she could tell Anna Victoria was a great instructor. She cared about her students, getting up once in a while to help them get into the right position or giving them tips and encouraging words, without being too *woo-woo*, which she hated.

The class itself was easy, though it was obvious many of the students were distracted. Anna Victoria had to call their attention a few times, because many of them had stopped to stare at a certain student in the back.

J.D. looked over at Sarah and caught her eyes when one of the poses had them facing to the rear of the room. Nodding at Thoralf, she whispered, "I'd run vagina first into that."

Sarah burst out laughing, nearly causing her to fall over. Anna Victoria sent them a warning look, but the corners of her mouth were tugging up, too.

Thankfully, the rest of the class went by without incident,

and by the time they got out of the *Savasana*, she felt relaxed and her mind refreshed.

"Thank you, everyone." Anna Victoria put her palms together. "Have a great day, and see you all next class."

"That was amazing," J.D. said as she rolled up her mat. "The yoga was good too," she chortled. "I can't believe Daniel would leave you alone with someone *that* hot."

She wrinkled her brow. "Why wouldn't he?" How much had Daniel told his friends about her? They didn't seem bothered by the fact that he'd been married to her all this time.

"I mean, you *know*." J.D. wiggled her eyebrows at Sarah

No, actually, she didn't. But before she could ask her what she meant, Anna Victoria and Thoralf approached them. "How was the class?"

"It was good, thank you so much, it was what I needed."

"You are an excellent teacher, my lady," Thoralf said. "My many thanks."

"What are you guys up to now?" Anna Victoria asked.

"Not much," she said. "We're supposed to meet Daniel and Adam at the pie shop for dinner at seven."

"Oh great, we'll join you," J.D. interjected. "Gabriel and Temperance will be there for sure anyway. Have you had pie before, Thoralf?"

"I confess, I have not," the dragon shifter said.

"I need to close up here," Anna Victoria said. "But do you mind waiting a couple of minutes? I'll have to call Damon, too, and have him meet us there."

"Sounds good. I'm gonna go change and meet you outside." She didn't mind J.D. and Anna Victoria joining them at all; in truth, it would be good to have more people around as a buffer. Whether she wanted them as a buffer between her and Adam or her and Daniel, she couldn't quite say.

Now that the initial exercise high was wearing off, her

thoughts strayed back to Daniel and what had happened in the bathroom yesterday. Her body still tingled at the memory of that orgasm and Daniel's mouth on her.

Fuck, he was fantastic at oral sex. Her eyes had nearly rolled to the back of her head when she came. Her knees went weak thinking of what actual sex would be like with him. Not that she would even get the chance to know.

Sex between them would just complicate things. It was already hard to stop her stomach from flip-flopping or her heartbeat from going a mile a minute when he was around, doing and saying things that made her hope for things she had no right to. *Besides, it wasn't like this was a permanent arrangement.*

Ignoring the pang in her chest, she finished cleaning up and headed outside. J.D. and Thoralf were helping close up, so she lent them a hand as well. Finally, they were done, and Anna Victoria locked up the studio. "We'll meet you Rosie's."

Soon, they were pulling up to the rear parking lot of Rosie's Bakery and Cafe. "You're in the back," the cheery proprietress said as soon as she and Thoralf entered. "I set up a table for you in the back, through the kitchen." She pointed at the door behind the counter. "Daniel told me you guys were eating here, and I didn't want anyone bothering you. Those damned media people are always sniffing around here, plus, I know even regular folks would be gawking at you guys, too."

"Thank you, ma'am," she said.

She chuckled. "Please it's just Rosie. Go on, Anna Victoria and J.D. are already in there."

Following her directions, they made a beeline to the display counter filled with pies and entered through the door behind it. To her surprise, it immediately led straight into the kitchen where a young woman was laying out a tray of pies on the table.

"... baby, that looks so good." It was Gabriel Russel, leaning over the counter, a hand reaching out.

"Gabriel!" she admonished, slapping his hand away. "They're still hot. You need to let them settle first."

"But I'm hungry now."

"You're always—oh, hello." The woman's face lit up when her light hazel eyes met hers.

Gabriel turned around. "Oh, hey, Sarah," he greeted. "You must be Thoralf," he nodded to the dragon shifter. "Daniel already told us you'd be here. This is my mate and fiancée, Temperance," he said, gesturing to the woman behind the table full of cooling pies.

"Hello," she said shyly. "Nice to meet you, Sarah. Thoralf."

Sarah did a double take, her eyes widening as they were drawn to the right side of Temperance's face. It was covered in scars, most likely from a burn. She recovered quickly though, and the other woman didn't seem fazed. "Nice to meet you too, Temperance." She took in a whiff. "Oh my God, that smells amazing. What pies are those?"

"I'm experimenting with some new flavors," she said. "These are honey lemon chiffon, chocolate ganache with almond crust, and salted caramel with mixed nuts."

"I want all of them, now," Gabriel demanded.

"Of course you do," she giggled.

"Hey, Sarah! Thoralf!" J.D. called. She and Anna Victoria were already seated at a table set up in the far corner. "Over here."

"Go ahead, and we'll serve these when they're done cooling," Temperance said, then turned to Gabriel. "Don't eat all of them, okay?"

They walked over to the corner, where two tables and several stools had been set up. "It's a tight squeeze, but we'll all fit." J.D. looked slyly at Thoralf and patted the empty seat next to her. "Come on, don't be shy. I don't bite ... hard."

Thoralf looked flummoxed and swallowed. "Um, I must confess, I'm not hungry yet. I must also check in with my ki—boss. I will see you at Daniel's home later tonight. If you ladies will excuse me." Turning on his heel, he headed out through the back door.

"*Aaaaand* shut down. Guess no Swedish sausage for me." J.D. pouted and planted her chin in her hands. "Did I come on too strong, do you think?"

"Why, J.D., I didn't even know you were open to dating," Anna Victoria said.

"*Pffft.*" She blew a stray strand of hair from her forehead. "If you come at me looking like that, I don't need dinner. I got my meal right *there.*" She waved her hand dramatically toward the door. "Do you guys even have eyes? Did you see all *that*?" Fanning herself, she let out a breath. "Man, what I wouldn't do to get horizontal under that. Maybe it's been too long since I got any action."

"Whatever you're looking for, you need to put yourself out there," Anna Victoria said. "The perfect guy isn't just going to land in your lap, you know."

"A hot guy with a foreign accent and biceps like boulders is exactly what I was looking for. Does Thoralf have a girlfriend?" J.D. asked Sarah. "Or a mate?"

"I don't think he's engaged," she answered, remembering what Gabriel called his fiancé. "But I don't know much about him, really. He just, uh, flew in two nights ago."

"No, I mean, a *mate,*" J.D. said. "Then maybe I'd understand why he's not into me."

"A what?"

The two women looked at each other. J.D. spoke up first. "You know, like—"

"Here you go," Gabriel interrupted as he put plates of pies down. "Just a couple of slices to start with. Temperance wants your opinion about what you think of these new flavors, though I already think they're fantastic. If you wanna order dinner now, let me know, otherwise, we'll wait for Daniel and Damon."

"Thank you," Sarah said.

"I'll wait," Anna Victoria said.

"All right, I'll be over there if you need me." Gabriel grabbed the empty tray and headed back to Temperance.

J.D. cleared her throat. "So, Sarah, I hope you don't think I'm too nosy, but you and Daniel—"

She sighed. "What do you guys know?"

"Absolutely nothing," J.D. said quickly. "Only that you guys got married over that weekend. I was there because it was Damon's bachelor party, and we've been best friends forever."

"And Damon is my husband and Daniel's boss," Anna Victoria added. "And he told me about you being married, but that's about it. Mostly it. I mean, Daniel's not the kind of guy who gives out details about his life."

"I know it's none of our business," J.D began. "But we're just ... curious, you know."

"And if you need anything, you can ask us," Anna Victoria offered.

Sarah knew she shouldn't be discussing her private business with them. They were practically strangers. But so much had happened since she came here, and she had no one else to talk to. "It's not what you think." She told them what happened that night, that both she and Daniel had been under the influence and couldn't remember anything, as well as their original plan of pretending to be married to avoid any scandal, and then quietly get an annulment once all the attention died down.

"Oh, wow," Anna Victoria said. "I had no idea."

"So ... you and Daniel ... you're just pretending? Like, nothing's happened between the two of you yet?"

"I—" She was going to deny it, then her face flushed when she remembered yesterday's encounter in the bathroom. The two women looked at each other and smiled. Damn, she wished her brain wouldn't short circuit each time she thought of Daniel Rogers's mouth between her thighs.

"Oh. My. God." J.D. exclaimed. "Something's happened! I knew it!"

Sarah buried her face in her hands. "It's not ... it's not that. Not that serious, I mean. Besides, we were just, uh, messing around. Caught in the moment."

"I don't know Daniel too well," Anna Victoria said. "But he doesn't seem like the type to just mess around with a girl if he's not serious."

"Sarah, he's seriously a good guy," J.D. added. "I mean, why not just see what happens?"

"What do you mean—"

The door that led into the dining room opened, and of course it was Daniel who walked in. "Hello?" he called. "Rosie said—" Immediately his silvery blue gaze landed on hers and a lazy smile spread across his lips. Those lips that were on her last night.

Heat spread from her belly to the rest of her body. Was he thinking of last night too? This morning, before Thoralf interrupted them in the hallway, she could have sworn there was a spark of *something* there.

"Holy shit," J.D. whispered. "Someone call the Blackstone Fire Department, because I'm about to spontaneously combust just being next to you two."

Oh God, am I that obvious?

Thankfully, before she could say anything else, Daniel—with Adam behind him—was already at their table. He introduced her brother to everyone and sat down on the empty chair beside her, pulling out the stool beside him so Adam could wheel in. "How was the class?"

"It was great." Tentatively, she leaned over toward Adam. "And the hike? Was it nice out there?"

His eyes lit up. "Oh, yeah," he said, nodding his head vigorously. "It was awesome! The trails went up so high and had these amazing views. Then we went to the station, and Daniel gave me a tour and told me all about the mountains! Did you know there are *dragons* around here?"

"I heard." She sent Daniel a knowing glance. "Did you see any?"

"Not today," Adam said. "But Daniel says he could find out when one of them is going to be out there and he'll take me to see them."

"That sounds, er, nice," she answered. While she didn't want to tell Adam they might not be around here for long, she didn't want to disappoint him, especially now that there was no more tension or animosity between them. Again, she looked at Daniel and gave him a grateful smile.

"Are those pies?" Adam's eyes went huge.

"Freshly-baked," she said, pushing a slice at him. "You guys must be hungry after that hike." She didn't need to encourage him as Adam began to demolish the piece of chocolate ganache pie.

"Hey, how about we order dinner?" J.D. suggested. "I'm starving. Hey, Gabe, stop smooching with our baker and take our dinner order! You're going to run Rosie's to the ground if you keep ignoring your customers."

"Hold your horses, McNamara," Gabriel called as he released Temperance, whom he had pinned up against the counter. He kissed her on the cheek.

Gabriel took their order, and soon they were served up some

heavenly savory dinner pies. Damon joined them in the middle of dinner, apologizing for being late as he had come from visiting a friend who lived far away.

"Are you all right?"

Daniel's voice made her shiver, his mouth so near her ear, she could feel his warm breath. She swallowed the pastry in her mouth. "Uh, yeah. Why?"

"You seem quiet, that's all." He put a hand on her knee. "Everything okay with you?"

"Of course." His hand was practically burning a brand on her skin, but she didn't want to push it away. "I just ... thanks. For whatever you said to Adam."

He shook his head. "I didn't say anything. I just took him up the trails and showed him around. No big deal."

But it was a big deal. She could see that the hike up the mountains had done Adam some good. She hadn't seen him laughing and chatting so easily in the last few months as he did now. And from the fact that every other word from his mouth was "Daniel said this" and "Daniel did that," she knew who to thank for that.

"But still ..." She placed a hand over his. "Thank you."

The gesture made something spark in his eyes, and she could have sworn she saw his Adam's apple bob up and down. "I—"

"Hey, is there a bathroom around here?" Adam asked.

Daniel quickly pulled his hand from under hers, a gesture that for some reason, made her stomach plummet. "Yeah, but it's in the main room, and that door swings in. Here," he said, standing up. "Let me get that for you. I need to go anyway."

Adam pushed himself away from the table with Daniel standing by, but not hovering over him nor trying to push his chair for him. Even when they approached the door, Daniel held it open, but allowed Adam to wheel himself out. Her heart skipped a beat watching the way he just seemed to genuinely care for her brother.

Something jabbed her in her side. "Huh?" She looked at J.D., who was grinning up at her maniacally.

"Oh, man," the other woman chuckled. "Don't tell me you don't want any of *that*." Her head cocked toward the door. "That's dinner, a movie, dessert, and breakfast the next day."

"I—" She covered her eyes with her hand. "It's complicated."

J.D. harrumphed. "Doesn't look like it to me. He wants you; you want him. You're already married. Would it be *so* bad?"

Excitement thrummed in her veins. *Would it?*

After dinner, they all lingered for a bit, staying to chit-chat—not to mention, J.D. told some embarrassing stories about Gabriel and Damon—but it was getting late, and Rosie needed to close up, so they all decided to go home.

"That was a good dinner," Sarah said to Daniel as they walked out into the parking lot of Rosie's. "Thank you for suggesting this."

"Well, we had to eat, right? And I don't think we can rely on Thoralf's kitchen skills for anything more complicated than pizza," he said with a chuckle. "Where's our friend by the way?"

"He said he had stuff to do, but he'd be back at the house. Oh, where's the SUV?" There were only a few vehicles left in the lot, and she didn't see the loaner from The Agency.

"Actually, I left it at home and brought this instead." He stopped in front of a red minivan. Taking a key-fob out from his pocket, he clicked on a button and the van's door slid open, then a ramp came out from inside.

"Thanks, Dan," Adam said as he rolled by them and into the

vehicle. The ramp automatically slid inside, and the door shut.

She looked at him, her mouth dropping open. "Where did you get this?"

"I uh, borrowed it."

"Where? How? Why?" The questions zinged in her mind, the words blurring together.

He shrugged. "Adam needed it, so I got it."

Damn you, Rogers. Did he have to be so ... so ... she couldn't even find the words for it. She wanted to shake his shoulders in frustration. Wanted to kick him in the shins. Wanted to knee him in the balls for making her feel this way. "Gah!"

"What—*mmm*!"

Her body had taken over, that was the only explanation as to why she threw herself at him and pressed her mouth to his. He stood there, frozen for half a second before he responded. His lips were warm, and she could still taste the traces of sugar, butter pastry, and coffee from their meal. When his hands came around her waist, she stepped away, pushing her palms against his chest. The look on his face was inscrutable. "I'll see you at home," she said. And like a coward, she scurried away to her car, quickly unlocking the door and hurrying inside.

Deep breaths, deep breaths. Her hands still shook as she stuck the key into the ignition. Lights flashed in the rearview mirror as she realized Daniel must be waiting for her.

How she even managed to pull out of the spot and drive all the way home, she wasn't sure. That kiss—the one she initiated —was still burning in her mind.

Would it be so bad?

The words repeated in her mind over and over again. He had responded to her kiss, but was he just being polite? *I shouldn't have done it.* But God help her, she didn't regret it at all.

She parked in the driveway and switched off the engine. As

Daniel parked, she waited for them to come out first. Adam exited the van, then Daniel rushed to the front door to unlock it. She followed, watching as Adam went in first, rolling his chair up the ramp and into the house while Daniel held the door open. As she passed by to follow her brother in, a hand landed on her arm.

"Hey."

She let out a breath. "Hey."

"Listen, can we—"

"Talk?" she finished. "Just, uh, come to my room later, okay?" Her heart thumped in her chest. "Let me go see to Adam first."

"All right. I should take a shower anyway."

"Okay." When he released her arm, she headed to the room Adam was staying in. The door was ajar, but she knocked first. "Adam?"

"Come in."

Pushing inside, she saw her brother coming out of the bathroom. "How are you?" she asked.

He rolled over to the bed. "I'm fine."

Padding over to him, she sat on the mattress so they could be at eye level. "Listen, Adam. I'm sorry you had to find out from the news and from those kids at school about me ... and Daniel."

He stared up at her with those soulful eyes, looking so much older than his sixteen years. "So, him and you ..."

"It's complicated," she admitted. "But you deserve the truth. Daniel and I aren't really married. I mean, legally we are, but we didn't mean to get married. We hadn't even met before that night." With a deep breath, she confessed to him about getting drunk and discovering her marriage to Daniel when applying for a loan.

"Yeah, I figured that was the case."

What? "You did?"

He nodded. "I saw the date of the wedding. Traced it back to the night you went out for Stephanie's bachelorette party. And, uh ... hacked the security cameras at the chapel. Man, you guys were trashed," he snickered.

"Yeah, we were. And it's embarrassing for me to admit that to you. That's why I couldn't explain it right away. And I didn't want you finding out."

"Really?" Genuine shock crossed his face. "You were embarrassed? But why?"

"Because I'm your older sister," she admitted. "And I have to be the adult you can depend on. Rely on. The one who you can trust will make the right decisions and protect you."

"You've been doing that for me and Darcey since we were kids. You don't have to do it forever. You shouldn't have to. And, well ... you deserve to be happy too."

"I *am* happy, Adam. With you guys. I don't regret any single moment we've all been together."

He flashed her a lopsided smile that made his dimples deepen. "I know. But, well ... you need to live your life too. And maybe you can find something of your own, you know?" He snorted as the tough, teen facade slipped back in. "That way you can stop hoverin' over me and Darcey."

"I do not—right." She pressed her lips together. "Anyway, you must be tired after the long day you've had. Do you need help getting to bed?"

"Ugh, *hovering*," he rolled his eyes. "But ... maybe you could just ... help me with the covers ... and stuff."

A lump grew in her throat, and she had to swallow it before she said, "Sure." She watched him lift himself up and get on the mattress, then helped him under the covers. After arranging them the way he liked it and tucking the ends under him, she said, "'Night, Adam."

"'Night, Sarah," he yawned.

Chapter 10

As Sarah slipped out of the room, her first thought was, *That went surprisingly well.* It was like a heavy burden had lifted off her shoulders now that she knew Adam wasn't mad at her anymore. He was growing up so fast, but it was nice that he still wanted her to do things like tuck him into bed, like she used to do when he was little.

Looking up at the stairs, a different feeling came over her. *Daniel.* They were going to have a talk. The door was closed to his room, so she went into hers.

This thing between them ... it was like a powder keg waiting to explode. And, well, she wanted it. Wanted to feel the heat, be consumed by it, even for just one night.

Because the truth was, she would rather have the memory of Daniel—a real one that her drunk brain wouldn't erase—and have her heart broken than have nothing of him to remember. Like Adam said, she needed to live her life too.

Would he want that? He wanted her; she knew that. But what if he'd changed his mind and decided he didn't want any complications.

As she mulled her options, she remembered that Daniel

could come by any second now and the room was a disaster zone as she hadn't cleaned up after getting all of the fall collection photographed. Various pieces of underwear were still spread out on the bed, and she quickly scooped them up to put away. However, an idea struck her as she remembered how Daniel reacted to seeing her in her creations last night. So, she headed into the bathroom, hands still full of silk and lace.

Designing lingerie wasn't just a job for her, but also a passion. She loved the feeling of wearing all those naughty things under her regular clothes, as they gave her a feeling of empowerment even while she walked around doing normal everyday stuff like going to the supermarket or to the bank. However, she'd never felt as powerful as she did yesterday when she literally brought Daniel to his knees. The thought of it made *her* knees weak again, but somehow, she managed to put on a silky blue bra with matching panties and stockings.

"Sarah? Are you in here?"

Her hearth thumped wildly in her chest. But she squared her shoulders and marched out of the bathroom before she lost her nerve. "Yes," she called out as she circled around the bed and sat on the edge, stretching one leg out in a pose that she knew would make her torso look longer. "Come in." Anticipation thrummed in her veins as the door swung open.

"Sarah, I wanted to—"

"Wanted to what?" she asked.

Daniel stood there, unmoving, his blue-gray stare practically burning a hole into her. "S-Sarah?" He muttered a curse under his breath.

Since he didn't make another move, she stood up and sauntered over to him, swaying her hips. "Yes, Daniel?" Though her hands shook, she managed to place them on his chest.

"Sarah." His eyes glittered and darkened with desire. "Do you really want this?"

"Yes." Her hands slid up to his shoulders. "I'm very sure."

A dark look passed over his face, making her shiver in delight. Before she knew what was happening, Daniel swooped her up into his arms and then deposited her on top of the bed reverently.

Her head spun from the heat coursing through her as he covered her body with his. She threaded her fingers through the still-damp hair at his nape, the smell of fresh soap on his warm skin tickling her nostrils as his mouth devoured hers. His hands roamed all over her neck and head, his fingers threading through her hair. He paused every few seconds to pull away and just look at her, as if he couldn't believe she was real and they were here, now.

She clawed at his shirt, helping him take it off as they continued to kiss and taste each other. He reached down and popped her breasts out of her bra, his hands kneading them and teasing the nipples to hardness.

He hauled her up so she sat on his lap, his cock straining against her. Reaching behind her, he unsnapped the bra and tossed it aside, his hands pushing her breasts together.

"Oh!" She moaned when he pinched her nipples. "Damn," she gasped when he bent down to suck one into his mouth. "Yes. Oh God." His tongue teased the tip as his mouth pulled on her tender nipple. Her hips rolled up into him, cradling him as she felt his erection brushing up against her core.

"God, I want you, Sarah," he confessed, planting kisses between her breasts and trailing up her neck.

"Daniel ..." She wanted him inside her so bad. "Please. Inside me."

He froze. "I wasn't prepared ... I mean ... I have condoms in my room. Let me—"

"No." She slid her arms around him. "It's fine. I'm safe." She knew the consequences of an unwanted pregnancy, so as soon as she turned sixteen, she got herself on regular birth control, not to mention still practiced safe sex. "And you ... you can't get any sicknesses, right?" Daniel would be the first she'd ever be with without any barriers.

"No. We can't. I ... Oh God." His eyes turned into twin silvery blue fire. "Baby doll ..." He kissed her hard before scooting backward. Her body ached in anticipation as she watched him push his sweatpants down, his cock springing free. She swallowed hard, watching the long, erect length of his dick, its purple-headed tip pointing at her. She'd seen it before, of course, when he had shifted back to his human form, and even then, she had thought it was impressive. But now ...

"Let me get you ready," he said.

She wanted to laugh and tell him she wasn't sure she could ever be ready for his giant dong, but yelped instead when he grabbed her and twisted her around, then settled her between his thighs. "Oh!" His mouth found the exact spot on her neck that turned her knees to jelly, suckling and nipping at it. His left arm braced around her, cupping her breast. Meanwhile, his right hand moved down her belly and slipped under her panties.

"Oh!" Her hips rolled against his fingers as he traced her slit. "Tease," she moaned when he refused to put it inside her. "Daniel," she mewled.

She could feel his smile against her skin as he slipped a finger in. One. Then another. "So wet already. Maybe you don't need too much help getting ready," he murmured. His thumb found her clit and flicked at it, making her shudder. "That's it, baby doll." He thrust his fingers inside her, in and out, the veins on his forearm straining. "Come for me."

Yes, sir.

Her body wracked with shivers as her pleasure tore through her. He didn't stop licking and sucking at her throat either as she rode his fingers to orgasm. Her mind went blank briefly, then came back down as her body sank against him.

"Good girl," he said, then slid his fingers up to her lips. "Taste yourself."

He thrust his finger into her mouth, and she sucked it clean. His eyes glazed over. "God, Sarah, I can't wait ..."

"Then don't," she moaned. "Get inside me."

It seemed he didn't need another invitation as he flipped her over, growling against her lips as he reached down between them. She lifted her hips to help him slip off the panties, but instead, he ripped them off. Though she wanted to protest because those samples were expensive, she couldn't bring herself to care, not right now. Not when his cock was pointed at her entrance, the head spreading her as he speared in.

"Dan—oh!" She clung to his shoulders, fingers digging into him as he pushed all the way in. God, she felt so full. Before she could put more thoughts together, he slid out, then back in again. And again. Slow, long strokes that had her purring like a cat.

A hand reached down between them, stroking her clit in a way that matched his thrusts. When he started speeding up, her breath came in faster pants, her body tensing as pressure built. Everything became fuzzy at that point as pure pleasure flooded her body, endorphins giving her a high she'd never felt before. As her body exploded in her second orgasm of the night, he pushed her further over the edge by giving her clit a hard pinch.

"Gahh!" Her body practically melted into the mattress. She felt like one of the clocks in Dali's painting. Just as her body began to recover, he hauled her up and flipped her over to her knees. "What—Daniel!"

His tongue thrust against her, licking at her soft folds. "You're fucking delicious," he murmured. "God, I could eat your pussy all day. Been dreaming about it since last night."

Ffuck, Daniel was a dirty bastard. It only made her hotter, knowing he had a sweet and nice facade, but was the total opposite in bed. Now she knew there was some truth to the saying that the nicest ones were the freaks between the sheets.

His tongue continued to tease and taste her, bringing her back to a near-orgasmic state but never quite getting there. When she let out an annoyed whimper, he spanked her ass. "Daniel!"

His hands gripped her hips, pulled back and she found herself impaled on his cock again. He smacked her again, this time even harder with a slap that echoed loudly in her ears. The stinging pain felt good, flooding her pussy even more.

Hauling her up, he shoved his fingers into her hair to force her back to arch. Damn if that didn't make her fucking wetter, if it were possible.

He began to thrust up into her, holding her body against his, his cock pushing deeper into her. "Feels ... so ... good ... inside you ..." he groaned. Without losing their connection, he pushed her forward. Her chest landed on the mattress and he hauled her ass upward as he continued to drill into her.

Hot damn, Rogers. His hand slid under her and found her clit again, and she knew she was done for. Even as her orgasm exploded, he continued to fuck into her, then let out a deep, long grunt. His body jolted, fingers digging into her hips as he unloaded his come into her, flooding her with his wet warmth.

Sarah felt like she was floating down from heaven. Again. A heavy weight pressed onto her, and when she let out a protesting groan, Daniel pulled away and out of her, the mattress dipping as he rolled to his side.

Feeling boneless, moving was the last thing she wanted to do right now. Not one inch. Maybe until tomorrow. Or next year. But as the high from her orgasm began to fade, she knew one of them had to move. Or say something. And if she didn't say what needed to be said, this might go on longer than it needed to.

With a sigh, she hauled herself up on her elbows, then peered over at him. His eyes were closed, reminding her of that morning she woke up next to him in the motel. However, this time, there was a small smile on his face. Slowly, she got to her knees and slid off the bed. At least she tried to, because in a split second, she found herself dragged backward as a strong arm slid around her waist.

"Where do you think you're going?" Daniel pinned her to the mattress, his teeth nipping at her throat.

"Maybe... um ..." Heat crawled up her face to the tips of her ears. "I didn't want to disturb your sleep. I can go to your room or the couch—*mmm*!"

He silenced her with his lips. "And why would you do that?" A hand snaked between them, pushing her legs apart.

"I thought you were tired and—oh!" *Jesus Christ, Mother Mary, Joseph, and all the saints!* His fully erect cock nudged at her, then began to slide inside. "Again?"

"*Hmmm-hmmm.*" He nuzzled at her neck. "Not. Tired," he said, giving her two hard thrusts. "Hope you can keep up, baby doll."

Mercy me. Those were her last thoughts as her eyes rolled to the back of her head.

Chapter 11

Daniel hoped he'd exhausted Sarah enough to stop her from attempting to get away. He'd felt her skittishness after the first time they had sex and feared she would bolt away if he didn't do anything to keep her in his bed.

Okay, so maybe sexing her into oblivion was a little extreme, but he was desperate for her to stay in his arms. She belonged there, and there was no way he was going to let her go.

Fuck, she was amazing. Most people had the notion that he was the nice guy, almost virginal even, but the truth was, he loved the kinky stuff in bed. Holding her down. Spanking that luscious ass. Pulling her arms back. And Sarah didn't seem to mind, and gave as good as she got. He groaned inwardly, thinking of that thing she did with her tongue that made his eyeballs nearly pop out of their sockets.

He stayed up to watch her, but slept lightly for what seemed like an hour or two. When he felt her shift and move, his eyes flew open. His gaze flittered toward the light filtering through the gaps in the curtains, indicating it was morning already. Sarah let out a raspy groan, then moved over toward the edge of the bed, so he reached for her again.

"Daniel," she warned. "I have to use the bathroom."

"All right," he said. "But you better come back soon."

She snorted, then crawled out of bed, but not before turning back at him and giving him a wink and smile. His mouth went dry, and his cock went hard as he watched her saunter into the bathroom naked, her hips swaying, and her ass jiggling. *Fuck.*

Minutes later, she came back and slipped into bed, cuddling up to him, one arm over his chest. He couldn't help but trace the ink over her skin. "This is beautiful," he said. Up close, he could see the finer details of the stained glass tattoo of the woman wearing a blue cloak dotted with yellow stars.

"A really talented artist did it back in Vegas. It's usually hard to get a good rendition of stained glass, but she did a great job."

"What is it, if you don't mind my asking?"

She tensed for a moment, but relaxed as he continued to soothe his fingers down her arms. "It's Our Lady of Guadalupe of Mexico," she said. "Supposedly, she appeared to a poor widower back in 1531 and made roses appear in his cloak."

"Does she have a special meaning to you?"

"Kinda. I can't remember much from ... from before I was found, but I do remember this image." Her eyes closed. "Looking up at it. And praying maybe. And a voice in my head of a woman whispering to me. I think ... I think she was my mother."

He slipped his arms around her and held her tight. "I'm sorry."

"What for?" She buried her face in his neck. "It was a long time ago. I don't even remember her."

"But you put this ink on you so you'll never forget."

Her breath hitched, then she muttered something unintelligible under her breath.

"What?" he asked.

"Nothing." Lifting her head, she propped her chin on his chest. "I mean, can we talk about something else?"

"*Hmmm* ... I can think of a few things." He grinned at her, one eyebrow quirking up. "Like where you got all those sexy panties. Have you been wearing them all this time?"

"Ha! Of course that's what you want to talk about." She slapped him playfully on the chest. "Actually, I should probably tell you. I mean, just so you don't think I'm a cam girl or something like that."

That thought never entered his mind. Not that he disapproved of that kind of stuff, especially if it was the woman's choice, but the thought of anyone seeing his mate on display made his stomach sour. His grizzly, too, did not like the idea of that.

"I design lingerie," she confessed. "And I sell it on my own website."

"Oh." He thought for a moment. "You made that? And the red one too?"

"I designed it, yes," she said. "I'm not trained or anything, but I taught myself how to draw and sew. After I put a concept down on paper, I'll make the prototype myself and send it down to a factory in Ecuador where they'll produce it. I was, uh, updating our website with the new collection when you burst into the bathroom."

"And you model it yourself?"

"Well, I don't have the money to hire models," she huffed, wiggling away from him. "And I edit out my head and my tattoos so no one knows—"

"Shhh ... baby doll." He hauled her back into his arms. "Don't get your feathers all ruffled. I'm not judging. In fact, I'm even more amazed."

"Amazed?"

"Between working your ass off and taking care of Adam and

Darcey, you found time to pursue your passion," he stated. "And, well, I hope you don't think this is trite, but I'm proud of you."

Lush lips parted. "P-proud?"

"Yeah." He kissed the top of her head. "For everything you've accomplished."

She squirmed uncomfortably.

"Now what?" he asked.

"Er, I should tell you ... once word got out about our marriage, my sales went through the roof," she said sheepishly. "See, I was getting a loan from the bank to open up my own shop when I found out we were married, and that's why I came here. Then when orders started pouring in ... that's kind of one of the reasons I wanted to stay here." She buried her nose in the sheets. "You hate me now, don't you?"

"Hate you?" How could she think that? "Never." Besides, it didn't matter to him why she stayed, only that she *did*. "Come here." He wanted to take care of her, make everything right for her.

"Daniel," she moaned when he kissed the side of her neck. "Oh ..."

He made love to her slowly, deeply, keeping her body pressed up against his, whispering sweet words of encouragement to her. When it was all done and he came deep inside her, he had to bite his lip to keep from saying those three words he'd been desperate to say to her. It wasn't that he didn't want to tell her, but it just didn't feel right yet. His grizzly, of course, was impatient. It wanted to bond with her, claim her.

Mating bonds were precious, as he'd seen firsthand with his parents. They had told him that in order for the bond to fully form, there couldn't be any barriers, and both partners had to be open to it. He could still feel some hesitation on her part, and though it pained him, he would wait for her. Forever if he had to.

"We should get up," she said, rolling over to her back. "Adam ... he might be hungry."

"Okay." He sat up. "But I'll make breakfast today. So ... what do you want to tell him?"

"Tell him? I've already told him the truth about what happened that night in Vegas."

"I mean, about us?" He gestured to the bed. "After all this. If you want, we can just act normal around him. And keep this between us." If Sarah wanted to keep this a secret from Adam for now, he would understand. He'd hate it, but would defer to her wishes.

"Oh." She shrugged. "He's sixteen, and Darcey had 'the talk' with him a couple years ago. You don't have to worry about things getting weird. Now, can you go make breakfast? I'm starving, and you're the one to blame for sapping my energy."

Relief poured through him. He didn't want to have to hide and sneak around, not with Sarah. And he liked Adam a lot and would hate to lose the teen's respect. He grinned goofily at her. "All right, breakfast it is."

As Sarah predicted, Adam didn't make a big deal or act weird when Sarah came down to the kitchen in her robe and cuddled up to him as he flipped pancakes or kissed him when he passed her a cup of coffee. In fact, if he didn't know any better, he could have sworn the teen looked almost smug.

After breakfast, Daniel hooked up the big screen TV in the living room, and they watched movies all afternoon, then ordered Chinese for dinner. There was no word from Jason or

Thoralf, and while Daniel felt a twinge of worry, he knew the dragon shifter was capable of taking care of himself.

That Sunday passed too quickly for Daniel's liking. Normally, he looked forward to heading into HQ and starting his week, but it was hard to leave Monday morning, especially with Sarah in his bed. Despite the night of lovemaking—and that quickie in the shower before he left—he still felt unsatisfied when he left her this morning. Maybe it was because both he and his bear longed for the mating bond, and until it was fully formed, they wouldn't feel at peace. He was tempted to stay at home with her, but sticking by her wouldn't make her any more ready to accept him as her mate, plus, he had people depending on him at work.

When he pulled into the parking lot of HQ, he was relieved to see that there were fewer people waiting outside, and there were no news vans trailing him, though that was probably because they didn't recognize the borrowed SUV. When he walked by the small crowd waiting outside, they spotted him and called to him. Today, instead of ignoring them, he stopped to chat and even took a few selfies before heading inside.

"Rogers, Chief wants to see you," the ranger at the reception desk called as soon as he got in.

"Thanks, Jansen." Whistling to himself, he headed for Damon's office and knocked on the door. "Hey, Chief. You needed to see me?" he asked as he poked his head inside.

"Daniel, come in," Damon said. "I'd like you to meet someone."

Striding inside, he closed the door behind him and approached his boss.

"Daniel, this is Dr. Cameron Spenser, our newest recruit," Damon introduced. "Cam, this is Daniel Rogers."

The man sitting in front of Damon's desk turned and stood up. He was an inch or two taller than him, his white-blond hair tied back in a ponytail. Iridescent blue-purple eyes behind a pair of gold-rimmed eyeglasses regarded him coolly. "How do you do?" His accent sounded British, and his voice cold and pure, like cut ice.

"Hey, Doc." Daniel offered a hand. "Nice to meet you."

Dr. Spenser looked at his hand like he was offering him poison, but when he didn't pull it back, the other man took it. "Nice to meet you. And it's Dr. Spenser, not Doc." His nose wrinkled. "Or Cam, if you prefer."

"Cam it is." His grip was strong, but Daniel didn't back down, returning it with a firm squeeze of his own. He could sense the other man's animal right away and smell the scent of fur. *Bear, definitely*. But it wasn't a grizzly like him or a Kodiak like Damon.

Damon cleared his throat, and both men released each other's hands at the same time. "Cam is coming in to replace Gabriel, at least until the new trainees come up to speed in the next year," he said. "I'd like you to show him the ropes until he gets his bearings."

"No prob. So, you're a doctor?" Daniel asked Cam. "And you came here to be a ranger?"

"I have my PhD in ecology, and conservation from the University of Basel," he said. "And my undergrad in botany, and zoology from Oxford."

"Nice," he said. "I studied forestry and wildlife conservation from Colorado State myself."

"Aside from doing ranger duties, Cam will be conducting some research on the wildlife here as well," Damon explained.

"It's part of our agreement," Cam continued. "Although ranger duties don't seem that hard. I doubt it will get in the way of my scientific pursuits."

Daniel could see why the chief chose him to give Dr. Uptight his orientation. That snooty, upper crust attitude would probably get him decked in no time by the other guys around here. "All right," he said. "Why don't we start with a tour of HQ, and then maybe you can join me on some trails?"

Damon looked relieved. "Thank you, Daniel."

"Let's go, Doc—I mean, Cam."

"Much obliged."

Daniel took him around HQ, giving him an extensive tour that took up most of the morning. Aside from the main building, the entire complex also including a garage for their vehicles, a storage area, holding areas, a dorm for trainees, and several empty cabins they used for different purposes depending on the time of the year. Afterwards, Daniel took him to the nearby trails.

"How about lunch?" he asked Cam as they were headed back. "Cafeteria's open, and the views are great."

"I've brought my own food," Cam replied. "And besides, I'm eager to set up my office and lab."

He shoved his hands into his pockets. "All right then, suit yourself. Just holler if you need me." *And don't forget to get rid of that stick up your ass.*

"Thank you." Cam gave him a curt nod and spun on his heels.

Glad that's over. Daniel mentally shook his head. A guy like that wasn't going to last around here, unless he wanted to spend all his time alone.

Seeing as he had time for lunch before he went on patrol, he made a beeline for the cafeteria. He ate alone, seeing as Gabe wasn't around anymore and Anders was back on night shift. Grabbing his phone, he meant to text Sarah, but remembered he didn't have her number on him. *Well, gotta take care of that tonight.* Maybe he could even convince her to take some selfies with him, so he could at least have pictures of her to look at and put on his phone as his wallpaper.

He glanced around, as if someone might accidentally look over his shoulder, and tapped on the browser icon on his screen. He searched for his name and pulled up the initial news story about their marriage. There were several pictures of him and Sarah coming out of HQ, including one with his arm around her, and her gorgeous face clearly seen. He zoomed and took a screenshot. *I'm one lucky bastard.*

He could stare at her the whole day, but he had a job to do. Reluctantly, he put the phone away, returned his lunch tray, and headed out the door.

According to the schedule board, his patrol would start in sector 8-F, which was a little farther up the mountain, but would allow him to hike up to the next ranger station in 10-G where he could catch a ride back to HQ when he was done. Transport picked him up and dropped him off at the southeast corner of 8-F.

He traversed the trails, checking in with HQ via radio every now and then as he kept his eyes and ears open for any signs of trouble. His main job as a Blackstone Ranger was to help out visitors—both human and shifter. Aside from being a private forest reserve, the mountains served as a sanctuary for the shifters who lived in town. Anyone was welcome to come up here and shift into their animal forms, as long as they stayed away from visitors and didn't cause harm to anyone. There was more than enough space for humans and shifters alike, and the public trails and campsites were only a small part of the vast area the mountains occupied. The shifters knew which places were just for them, as the rangers marked them with special paint that only they could see, carved symbols on the tree trunks, or sprayed a signature scent that could only be detected by their keen noses.

As he got farther up, he knew there would be less people and shifters, too, as it was quite far to go on foot. This was one of the best parts of the job for him—being outside in nature. He had so many good memories of being up here in grizzly form with Pops, or hiking the trails with his parents and camping out in the woods in the summer. He wondered if Sarah was an outdoorsy person and if she would enjoy coming up here for the weekend with nothing but a tent.

The buzz of his walkie-talkie knocked him out of his reverie. "Grizzly One, this is Base. Are you there? Over."

He pulled out the portable radio from the holster on his waist and clicked the call button. "This is Grizzly One. I hear you loud and clear, Base. Over."

"Grizzly One, we have a lost hiker last seen in sector 8-L. Human female, thirteen years old, red hair, last seen wearing khaki shorts and a green T-shirt. Wandered off from her parents. Over."

He wasn't too far from that area, but he doubted a young girl could make it all the way up here. "All right, Base, I'll keep a lookout for her. Over."

"Thanks Grizzly One. Over and out."

Once the crackling of his radio faded, he was again surrounded by silence. He tuned his ears carefully, but there was nothing around him except the chirping of birds and a rustle here and there of small creatures scurrying about, so he continued on his patrol.

His shift seemed so much longer today, and the sun was still high, which meant he had hours to go. As he crossed over to sector 10, he stopped and sat on a rock and unscrewed the top of his water bottle.

A sudden noise from his left made him freeze, the bottle halfway to his lips. Every single hair on his body rose, and his grizzly stood up on its hind legs, paws raised. Blood roared into his ears as he dropped the bottle, shot to his feet and turned toward the source of the sound. "Who—fuck!"

An arm grabbed him from behind and then jabbed something in his throat. *Goddammit!* The dizziness that passed over him told him what was injected into his system. He managed to pull away, his hands clawing at his skin as if that would stop the bloodsbane from doing its work.

"Finally caught you, animal scum."

That voice. It was the same one from the night of the attack. *Lord Nox,* he recalled. "Wha-what do you want?" He fought the bloodsbane working into his system, but he could feel his muscles start to relax, and his head felt light. His grizzly swayed back and forth, confused as to what was happening.

Don't let it get to you! Fight it.

Injecting bloodsbane had a different effect from digesting it. Being injected into the bloodstream, the drug would take effect much faster. And depending on how much they put into him, it could knock him out cold from a few minutes to a couple of hours.

"Vermin," Nox sneered. "We'll exterminate you soon." Several people dressed in black slipped in through the trees, and formed a semi-circle around him.

"Are you going to kill me?" Daniel slurred. "What—"

A cry cut him off. Swinging his head around, he saw one of Nox's minions holding something in his arms. Or someone, wearing a green T-shirt and brown shorts. *The lost kid!* "Goddamn you, let her go! You want me, right? Take me, I won't fight you. Just leave her alone. What do you want a kid for, you pervert?"

Nox laid his palm on his chest in a mocking, shocked gesture. "Me, hurt a human child? Never!" A slow smiled spread across his mouth. "You, however ... well, we all know shifters have a base animal instinct they can't control. What's to say *you* won't attack her?"

"I'd never hurt a kid!" What the fuck was going on here? Daniel lunged at him, but only staggered forward.

"Maybe not her, but then maybe you'd kill someone to protect her, won't you, hero?" Nox sneered. "And when the media sees footage of you attacking a poor human trying to defend this girl, and then she ends up dead, well ... we'll let the media decide how to spin the story."

"Fuck you!" So that was their game. Frame him for an attack against humans. "You'll never ... never ..." He dropped to his knees, the edges of his vision growing dark.

"I'll never what?" Nox laughed. "Get away with it? Of course I will. And what sweet revenge this is. In fact, it's better than our original plan of assassinating Baker. The world will finally see what truly vile and disgusting creatures you are. Once you wake up, you better be ready for your close-up, hero. You will fire the first shot that starts the war."

War? What—

But he didn't have the chance to finish his question as the world blacked out.

Chapter 12

Sarah couldn't concentrate while working from the house that day. Everything about the place reminded her of Daniel, and she found herself missing him. It sounded pathetic, but she couldn't help herself. *He's going to be back tonight, no need to mope.*

"Ugh." She'd been staring at the same photo for ten minutes and hadn't done a thing. Burying her face in her hands, she groaned. It would be a couple more hours until he came back. His shift was until nine o'clock, which meant he wouldn't be home until ten. If only she could contact him. Call him. Hear his low, sexy baritone. They hadn't even exchanged numbers, so she couldn't even do any of that.

Ew, stop acting like a teenager in love.

Her heart went pitter-patter at the thought. Love? Was she in love with Daniel? Wasn't it too early? Did he feel the same? Her stomach fluttered excitedly. *Whoah, cowgirl! It's definitely too early to feel this way.*

"Arggh!" She slammed her tablet facedown on top of the kitchen table. "Adam!" she called out to her brother, who was in the living room watching TV. "Get your stuff together! We're going to Rosie's!"

It hadn't been hard to convince Adam to come with her to Rosie's. He'd been moaning about the poor reception and lack of high-speed Internet at Daniel's house all day. So, they packed up the borrowed minivan and headed down to Main Street. Rosie was only too happy to see them and sat them in a booth in the back where she could work on editing her photos and Adam could play on his phone.

"Here you go." Rosie placed two pieces of cherry pie on their table. "Enjoy, kiddos," she said as she sashayed away.

"I'm starving," Adam said as he proceeded to devour the slice in front of him.

"You're always starving," she said wryly.

"I'm a growing boy," he said through a mouthful of buttery pastry. "Man, I don't think I've had pie this good back in Vegas."

"I'm sure we can find something just as good when we get home," she assured him. A pang in her heart came from nowhere at the thought of going back to Vegas.

Adam swallowed and washed everything down with a gulp of water. "So," he began. "Are you and Daniel ... I mean, are you like, a thing now? Cuz you guys have been acting like you are."

She was about to dig into her slice, but his question made her pause. When Daniel had asked her yesterday if they should act like nothing happened between them in front of Adam, something inside her immediately protested. She told herself it was because she had vowed to never keep anything from Adam so he wouldn't lose his trust in her again. But now, she wasn't sure if that was the *only* reason.

"Sarah?"

"Sorry." She put her fork down. "I don't want to lie to you, Adam," she began. "I promise you from now on, I'll tell you what's going on. But the truth is ... I don't know."

"Oh." His gaze dropped to the tabletop. "I mean, if you are, I wouldn't mind. Daniel's a great guy. And you deserve to be with someone who treats you right. And ... and ..." He twiddled his fingers together on top of the table. "I want you to know, you don't have to worry about me and Darcey. We'll be fine on our own, okay? I know I can get a scholarship when I graduate in two years, just like we always planned. My guidance counselor says my grades might even be good enough for MIT. I just have to keep working hard and enroll in more AP classes."

Her throat burned at Adam's words, and she reached out to cover her hands with his. "Adam, I would never leave—" The sound of the front door crashing as it hit the wall cut her off. "What the—Thoralf?"

The dragon shifter, dressed in full armor, stood at the entrance, his eyes scanning the room until they landed on her. "Sarah!" He strode over to them. "Is Daniel with you?"

"Daniel?" A pit began to form in her gut. "No, he's at work. What's up?"

His expression darkened. "I'm afraid ... I'm afraid that The Knights may have a plan for him. And my sources say they will act on it today."

"A plan?" Blood drained from her face, and the pit in her stomach grew.

"Sarah?" Adam asked. "What's he saying? And what the heck are you wearing, Thoralf?"

"Hey, what's going on out here?" Gabriel had rushed into the dining room, and stopped short when he saw Thoralf. "Whoa, dude, what's with the costume? And that sword ... careful you don't cut your leg off with that thing."

"It is my armor and weapon—" he began.

"He thinks Daniel might be in danger," Sarah interjected.

"Danger?" Gabriel's face turned serious. "Okay, hold on. What do you mean, in danger?"

Thoralf sighed. "I am not Daniel's friend from college. I am Thoralf, former captain of the Royal Guard of the Northern Isles—"

"Someone tried to kill Daniel the other night, and Thoralf was there to save us," Sarah blurted out. "And Jason Lennox and his wife run some kind of secret shifter agency that fights the bad guys. Now, can we get to the part where Daniel's life is in danger?"

Gabriel's blue eyes grew round as he processed the information. "Jason Lennox ... agency ... what now?"

Panic made her patience run thin, but if Daniel was in danger, they had to act now. "Please, Gabriel. He's at work. But I think he's in trouble." Something inside her was telling her that something was very wrong. "Can you check on him?"

"Already on it." Gabriel had his phone to his ear. "Hey, Damon, can you check on Rogers for me? When did he last call in to base?"

As each second ticked by, Sarah's chest contracted. Oh God. What if Daniel was dead? *No. Can't think like that.* Daniel was alive. She didn't know how she knew, but she just did.

Though she couldn't hear the other side of the conversation, from the way Gabriel's brows drew together and his lips pulled back, she knew it wasn't good news. "Couple hours, huh? Can you—yeah, thanks, man."

"What did he say?" Sarah asked as Gabriel tucked his phone back in his pocket.

"Daniel was out on patrol, but hasn't checked in with Base for a couple hours now." Gabriel's mouth drew back in a tight smile. "I'm sure he's fine. Maybe he just forgot or got busy with a rescue."

"No." She shook her head vehemently. "There's something wrong. I know it."

He flinched. "*Crap.*"

"What's wrong?" Thoralf asked.

Gabriel's expression became inscrutable. "If she says something's wrong, then Daniel really is in trouble."

"You believe me?"

"Unfortunately, I do." He massaged his temples with his fingers. "She's Daniel's mate."

Thoralf's eyes bugged out. "Fated mates! How glorious. We can all only hope to find that who is the other half of our souls."

"M-mates?" she repeated. "What do you mean? We weren't even engaged. Is that what happens when you get married to a shifter?"

"No, no." Gabriel blew out a breath. "See, most shifters have a mate, one that they're meant to be with. Call it soulmates. When we find our mates, we form a kind of metaphysical bond with them. You and Daniel are mates, and his bear recognized you the moment he saw you."

"But Daniel ... he never said anything."

"We told him to tell you," Gabriel said.

"But he didn't want to," she finished. *Daniel didn't want to tell her they were soulmates.* An ache formed in her chest. *Why?*

"Wait, Sarah, it's not what you—"

"Apologies," Thoralf interjected. "But time is running out. If The Knights have him, then we must act quickly."

Daniel was in danger. Every nerve in her body told her it was true. Her throat burned at the thought that maybe he didn't want to be with her, but that would have to wait until later. She couldn't let him die. "We need to go find him."

"Stay here, Sarah, and await for word," Thoralf said. "I will go and scour the mountains for him." In a flash, Thoralf disappeared.

"Holy fucking shit!" Adam shouted. "Did you guys see that?"

"Adam, watch your mouth," she admonished.

"Are you fucking kidding me? He just vanished into thin air! What the fuck am I supposed to say?"

She buried her face in her hands. *Daniel, please be okay.* What could those evil Knights be doing to him now? *Well, I can't just sit around and do nothing.* Squaring her shoulders, she turned to Gabriel. "Will you take me up there? To the mountains?"

"What?" Gabriel looked at her incredulously. "No way. Daniel'll kill me if I put you in any danger."

"Please, Gabriel." She was desperate to know what was happening. "I know I won't be able to go out and help, but I need to know. I *need* to be there." She didn't know why, but her heart was ready to burst out of her chest at any moment. "What if it was Temperance? *Please.*"

He hesitated for a moment. "All right. I know where he's supposed to patrol and we can make most of the way up there in my Jeep. We'll have to check in with Damon first."

"Sarah?" Adam asked in a quiet voice. "Are you really going up there?"

"I have to," she said. "I need to." Despite the looming thought that Daniel didn't want to be mates with her, she knew she had to see this through. She needed to see him safe, and then ... then she'd let him go.

Adam looked like he wanted to protest but then squeezed her hands. "You stay safe, Sarah."

She grabbed her purse and kissed him on the forehead. "I will. See you when I get back."

Chapter 13

Daniel didn't know how long he'd been out. The bloodsbane had knocked him out, but as his body fought its effect, he found himself in some kind of half-dream, half-awake state. He was aware of voices around him and dark shapes, the feeling of being carried and dragged around, but his brain couldn't make the proper connections to tell him what was going on. As the drug ebbed away in his system, a pounding headache took its place. His grizzly tore up at him, prodding him to get up. A groan tore at his scratchy, dry throat.

"... waking up. Get ready."

His eyes flew open, then quickly shut as light penetrated his corneas. Slowly, he opened them up again. At first, everything was fuzzy. In no time, as his shifter metabolism got rid of the remains of the bloodsbane, his vision cleared up.

They were in some sort of clearing, surrounded by trees. A campsite, it looked like, as he saw some picnic tables a few feet away. He didn't recognize this one, but from the subtle scent in the air, he guessed they were in a shifter-only area of the mountains. Probably Campsite Sigma in Sector 12.

"Ah, here we are. Get up, you beast."

"Beast?" he slurred. "I'll show you—" *Fuck!* Something prevented him from moving his arms, and try as he might, he couldn't free his limbs. "Bastards," he spit out. They had tied him down with chains. "This isn't going to hold me." He struggled to his knees as his grizzly prepared to take over their body. The shift alone would be enough break free of the metal links.

"I know," Nox answered. "And it's not supposed to. Get that camera ready," he hissed to someone behind Daniel.

"Motherfucker!" He reined back his Grizzly. It roared at him, wanting to break them free. *No, we can't let them film us.* Nox's words from earlier came back to him. They were planning to film him killing a human. But how?

The girl. His keen senses picked up the soft cries and sniffles. His head snapped toward the source somewhere on his right. There she was, a few feet away, crumpled on the ground, her hands tied behind her as tears poured down her cheeks. Big blue eyes looked at him, the terror unmistakable.

"Myers," Nox called. "Are you ready?"

A man in a plaid shirt and khaki pants walked up to him. "Yes, Lord Nox."

"You're making a great sacrifice to the cause," Nox said. "Your name will be celebrated in the history books."

"I am honored to make this sacrifice, Lord Nox. For our cause. For The Knights."

A chill ran down Daniel's spine. This man ... they were going to sacrifice him. To Daniel's grizzly. "Bastards!" he scream. "I won't kill him."

"If you don't, then the girl dies," Nox said. "Kill her, Myers."

"Yes, Lord Nox." He bowed deeply, then removed something dangling from his belt. Something shiny that glinted when light from the setting sun caught it. A knife.

Daniel swallowed, watching as Myers approached the girl.

Her eyes grew wide, and she froze as she saw the knife, her mouth forming an O. A scream ripped from her mouth as Myers drew closer.

"C'mon now, hero," Nox taunted. "Are you going to let him kill her?"

"Fuck you!" he spat. "I won't be part of your games." He lowered his voice so the girl wouldn't hear him. "You're going to kill her anyway." She would be a witness, after all.

"Yes, but Myers can make it a long, agonizing death," Nox cackled. "And you'll watch every minute of it. Now, you can watch while he slices her up, or you can kill him now, and I promise I'll make it quick for the both of you."

Hope drained from within him. There was no winning this. The only way he could save the girl was to kill Myers, but that's what Nox wanted. Or he could watch that butcher cut up an innocent girl.

I have to at least try.

Letting out a deep roar, he called on his grizzly. It was only happy to oblige, and his muscles rippled and his limbs stretched out.

"Start filming!"

Sharp teeth grew from his mouth and fur sprouted all over his body. As his shoulders and torso swelled, the chains strained, the sound of metal breaking apart ringing through the forest. *Just one more—*

A pained shout tore through the air. But it wasn't the girl.

What the hell?

A great big brown blur whizzed past him and barreled straight into Myers, knocking him down. He didn't know what it was, but something about it was familiar. Then, something shimmered in the corner of his eyes. Sunlight glinted off gold metal.

Thoralf!

Dressed in his full armor, the dragon shifter swung his sword as he sliced through two of Nox's minions. Another tried to get him from behind, but Thoralf easily evaded them and ran his weapon through the attacker's stomach.

"What the hell—get them!" Nox sputtered.

Daniel wasted no time as he finished his shift, his grizzly's body completely breaking free of the chains. As he charged toward Nox, from the corner of his eye he saw the remaining goons point their guns at Thoralf. Instantly, scales rippled from his body, and the bullets bounced off him.

"No!" Nox screamed indignantly. "Damn you—"

But the grizzly landed on top of him, full of rage as it dragged its long claws down his face. The metallic smell of blood tinged the air, and Nox's screams of pain echoed through the woods. Another paw came down, ripping at his chest and piercing through the Kevlar. Finally, the grizzly's giant maw opened up and went straight for the man's throat.

The warm trickle of blood in their mouth made Daniel want to gag, but the grizzly was in charge. Only when Nox's body stopped twitching and convulsing did it let go. It got up and backed away, lumbering around to check their surroundings for more danger.

It seemed they had gotten rid of all of Nox's men as there were no more of them around. Not alive, anyway. Myers's bloody body lay on the ground, his torso shredded in a similar manner to Nox's. There had been another bear who had come in, but who was it?

"Daniel, are you all right?"

The grizzly swung around and roared at the dragon shifter.

Thoralf chuckled. "I'm sorry, my friend, that it took so long to come and rescue you. The mountains were much vaster than I initially thought. It was a good thing I came across your bear friend, and he deduced where you could be."

Bear friend? But that other bear wasn't Damon or anyone else that smelled—

Krieger.

John Krieger was one of the five men he'd gone into the ranger training with five years ago. He'd been a quiet guy, mostly kept his head down and did all the exercises without complaint. The old chief had assigned him a permanent position up near Contessa Peak, and as far as Daniel knew, he mostly stayed up there.

"Are you unharmed?" Thoralf asked.

He nodded, but of course he didn't see that. He was fine but —the girl! Quickly, he pushed his grizzly back down, shifting back to his human form. "There's a girl," he managed to say as he took in a big gulp of air. "She's—" Glancing back, he saw that she was still there on the ground, but it looked like she had passed out.

"I'll see to her," Thoralf offered and rushed toward the prone form.

"Jesus." He raked his hand through his blood-soaked hair. Adrenaline was still pumping in his veins, making him jittery. Hopefully there would be no more surprises.

However, the wind picked up, making the trees shake all around them. The sound of wings flapping made him look up to the sky.

"Oh, fuck!" *Spoke too soon.* "Ack!" He was blinded again as something gold flashed above him, slowly getting larger. Two giant clawed feet landed with a thunderous thud, making the ground shake. The fifty-foot golden dragon stood there for a moment, shaking its mighty wings before it began to shrink. Soon, Jason Lennox's naked form stood in its place.

"Daniel—Jesus!" His silvery eyes bugged out as Daniel's blood-covered form greeted him. "What the hell happened?"

"The Knights," he said. "They took me. And a hiker," he

nodded toward Thoralf, who was untying the girl's bonds. "Long story. But we took care of them."

Jason winced at the carnage around them. "Yeah, you did. Fuck, I'm gonna have a whole bunch of paperwork to fill out." He raked his hands through his hair. "I—shit. They're here." The sound of engines drew closer.

"Did you bring backup?" Daniel asked, and Jason answered with a nod. "And by the way, how did you find me if you weren't with Thoralf and Krieger?"

"Damon called me when you didn't check in while doing your rounds," he answered.

"But how did he know I was in trouble?"

"It was Sarah," Jason said. "Apparently Thoralf was looking for you and she figured out there was something wrong and called Damon. She blew our cover, but I understand. She's your mate; of course, she's worried about you."

"How did you know she's my—never mind." Damon probably told them.

"Speaking of which," Jason said. "She'll be here anytime now."

"Wait—she's coming here?"

"Of course. She raised hell when we wouldn't let her come. Threatened to expose us, then sue the rangers and me for every penny I got until I let her in the truck." Jason removed a drawstring bag hanging from his shoulder, opened it, and tossed Daniel something which he caught. "Brought you some extra shorts. You'll want to wash up before your reunion."

He glanced down at his blood-covered body. "Right." He moved stiffly as he made his way to the edge of the clearing to a small brook just outside the campsite. Quickly, he washed himself with the cold mountain water as best as he could and then slipped the shorts on before heading back.

The clearing was starting to fill with people from The

Agency. He saw Thoralf talking to Jason and one of the female agents wrapping a blanket around the girl, and he sighed with relief. However, when he saw a familiar figure sitting at one the picnic tables, he tensed once again. *Sarah.*

She'd been worried for him. Believed that he was in danger without any hesitation. And she'd even fought a Blackstone dragon so she could come and rescue him. If that didn't mean she was ready to be mates, he didn't know what else would prove it.

His heart hammered as he pivoted in her direction, his steps picked up as he approached her. All he wanted to do was hold her in his arms and kiss her. And tell her he loved her with all his heart.

She must have sensed his approach, because her head lifted. The sight of her velvety brown eyes growing wide pinned him to the spot. "D-Daniel." Her lower lip trembled. "I—" She sucked in a quick breath. "You're ... okay."

"I sure am," he said, his voice hoarse as emotion welled up.

She gave him a curt nod. "All right then."

All right then? That didn't sound like the warm reception he was expecting.

Standing up, she smoothed her palms down on her jeans. "I'm glad. And that it's all over."

"All over?" he echoed.

"Yeah. The Knights ... they're gone, right? They're not a danger to you anymore."

"I suppose." Nox and his men were dead, and the hiker was safe.

"Good." Her shoulders did a little shrug. "Well, I guess that means me and Adam and Darcey aren't in danger either."

"I guess."

"Great. I'll catch a ride back with the agents, and I can go pick up Adam."

"Pick up Adam?" *What the hell is she saying?*

"We'll grab our things from your house and head back. Christina offered the use of their private jet." The corner of her lips turned up, but her eyes remained dull. "Adam will be thrilled."

Numbness spread in his chest, down to his limbs, making it difficult to speak.

She cleared her throat. "By the way, I'll file the paperwork first thing tomorrow when we get back."

"Paperwork?"

"Yeah, the annulment papers."

The words were like knives twisting in his gut. He stared at her, not saying anything or moving, as if that would slow down the world crumbling around him.

She stood there, her lips pursed together for what seemed like eons. "All right then. Have—have a good life, Daniel." Quickly, she pivoted on her heel and rushed off.

He stared after her, dumbfounded. "Have a good life?" he repeated.

What. The. Fuck.

"Sarah!" He called after her. When she didn't stop or turn back, he finally found the strength to pry his feet from where they were frozen to the ground and tore after his mate. It only took half a second to get in front of her. "Sarah! Wait!" He grabbed her arms. "Sarah ... Sarah, look at me," he urged, gripping her tighter when she turned her head away and tried to squirm away. "Please."

Chocolate brown eyes glittered with unshed tears, and he felt his heart crack. "Let me go, Daniel."

"Let you *go*?" The forcefulness of the last syllable made her flinch. "I can't, Sarah. I can't let you just walk out of my life."

Her jaw tightened as two tears tracked down her cheeks. "You don't want me around."

"Don't want you—" He wanted to shake her, but stopped himself. "What the hell makes you think that?"

"Because you didn't tell me I was your *mate*!"

Oh, shit. How did she—

"I had to find out from *Gabriel*," she spat.

"Fuck. That's not how—"

"It's all right," she said, her shoulders sinking. "I just ... I understand. This was all temporary. And getting married was a drunken mistake. We shouldn't have—"

This time, it was his grizzly who answered with a roar of denial. It rattled through his chest and ripped through his throat so loudly, it made Sarah snap her mouth shut. "I don't know where you got that idea, but you're wrong."

Her nostrils flared. "Then why didn't you tell me? Gabriel said you didn't want to."

"Not *yet*." His chest ached with desperation as he felt her about to slip from his fingers. All because he didn't tell her right away. "You weren't ready to hear it. If you were a shifter it would have been easier. You would have known right away, like I did." He took a deep breath and took her hands into his. "I think ... that night we met, someone roofied my drink. It's a special drug that only affects shifters. But right before I took it, I saw you and recognized who you were to me. But the drug made me forget, for the most part.

"I woke up the next day, and there were flashes. For months, I could feel something was wrong with me, but I didn't know what. Then you came here and found me, and I knew it right away. I wanted you right then and there. I concocted that plan to fake our marriage, though I knew it was wrong. But then you walked back into HQ and told me you wanted to stay, well, I went along with it, but all this time, I've been trying to find ways to win you over."

She double-blinked. "Win me over?"

"Yeah." He rubbed the back of his head with his palm. "I wanted you to *want* to stay because of me. Not because of some publicity stunt. But the mating thing is complicated enough as it is. I didn't think you felt the same yet, not with the same intensity as I did. Mates, you see, once they're ready to open up to each other, they form a bond. One that's unbreakable and links them for life. I wasn't sure that you were even open to that, and I wanted to give you time. I'm sorry, Sarah. I messed this all up."

"Y-you wanted to give me time?"

"Yes," he said. "To fall in love with me the way I fell in love with you."

Her jaw dropped. It looked like she wanted to say something, but she sucked in a breath instead.

"Sarah? Are you all—"

"I love you," she blurted out as her cheeks reddened. "Oh God. Daniel. I love you."

"Sarah ..." His arms encircled her as he pulled her to him, bending his head to kiss her.

Daniel always thought that the first time he kissed his fated mate, he'd hear trumpets blaring in the background, fireworks blasting, or a choir of angels sing. But he'd already kissed her several times, and there had been no such music in his ears.

But this kiss ... well, it would certainly give all the angels in heaven a run for their money. Music filled his ears, like the sweetest symphony on earth. It spread through him, warming him from the top of his head to the tips of his toes as he felt something tighten around his chest, but in a good way. He pulled away from her in surprise. "Sarah ... I think ..."

"Did we bond?" she asked.

He nodded. "I can feel you." Taking her hand, he placed it on his chest. "Right here."

"Me too," she whispered.

"I love you, Sarah." He kissed her knuckles. "My mate. Will you stay with me? Here in Blackstone? Or I can move to Las Vegas. I don't care where we live, as long as we're together."

She shook her head. "No, I can't ask you to do that," she said. "I can do my work from anywhere, but you can't. I'll move here."

"Really?" He whooped in joy and lifted her up, spinning her around. "You won't regret it." He kissed her hard. "You'll love living here. So will Adam. Lucas Lennox High has a great computer science program. He'll get into MIT for sure and—"

"Wait, what?" Her eyebrows knitted together. "Adam? Here? In Blackstone?"

He nodded vigorously. "Of course. I've thought this through. He'll live with us. Your sister, too. Blackstone's a shifter town. Darcey'll fit right in. And you can open your store here."

"I ..." A choked cry escaped her mouth as her eyes filled with tears.

"Baby doll, don't cry." He wiped at her cheeks with his thumbs.

"These are tears of happiness, silly" she said with a laugh. "I can't believe that you'd want them with us."

"Of course." His grizzly chuffed with indignation at the thought that Adam and Darcey would live anywhere else but within their den. "You're mine, Sarah. And that means they belong to me too. Mine to protect and watch over."

"I ... I don't know what to say. Th-thank you."

"No need for that," he said. "Just say you'll be with me, forever."

"Yes," she whispered. "Forever."

Chapter 14

Sarah couldn't wait to get out of the mountains, and she knew Daniel felt the same way, thanks to their bond. Though Jason wanted them to come down to The Agency headquarters for a round of interviews and debriefing, Daniel quickly vetoed that idea explaining that he and Sarah were both mentally and physically exhausted from their ordeal, plus Adam was all alone back at Rosie's. It was a good thing Jason understood, plus, Thoralf had promised to stay and finish the cleanup and debrief in their stead.

They picked up Adam back in town. The relief on the teen's face was obvious as they entered Rosie's, though he later claimed that it was allergies that made his eyes water, and he certainly was *not* crying.

"God, I can't wait to get in bed," she sighed as they neared the house.

"Me neither," Daniel said, but wiggled his eyebrows at her.

"Eww," Adam groaned. "Gross. I think I'm going to hurl some mango tango peach pie all over your upholstery. Please keep it down tonight, I don't want to hear what my sister sounds like when she's banging."

"Language!" Sarah warned.

Daniel laughed. "We'll try to keep it—oh, *fuck* me."

Adam snorted. "Nice mouth you got there, Rogers. Careful your mate doesn't wash it out with soap."

"Daniel?" Her head cocked to the side as he muttered something unintelligible. "What's wrong?" she asked as they pulled in front of the house. The car stopped, and he cut the engine. "Why aren't you going into the driveway? Adam needs —oh." There was another vehicle parked in their usual spot. Actually, it was the same kind of minivan they were using, only in blue. "Are you expecting guests?"

"Not really." His hands flexed and un-flexed around the wheel, then he let out a sigh. "C'mon, I'll introduce you guys."

"Introduce us?" But Daniel had already slipped out of the driver's seat.

"What's going on?" Adam asked from the back seat.

"I don't know," she shrugged. "Are you okay back there? Need my help?"

"Nah, I can get out on my own. You go ahead and see what's happening."

Sarah got out and jogged over to where Daniel stood next to the other minivan. The driver's side door opened, and a tall man stepped out, snakeskin cowboy boots landing on the asphalt, his face obscured by a Stetson hat. When he lifted his head, she found herself staring into a pair of silver-blue eyes. "Hello there, pretty lady," he drawled. "Or should I call you, daughter-in-law?"

"Hey, Pops," Daniel greeted. "This is a surprise."

Pops? Sarah looked from their unexpected visitor to Daniel, then back again. Except for the weathered skin and thick white mustache, the older man held a close resemblance to Daniel.

White bushy eyebrows drew together. "Not as surprised as we

were when we heard the news." His words held a touch of reproach, reminding her of the tone she used on Adam when he was a kid and had done something naughty. "I know it's our choice to live off the grid and avoid the damned news like the plague, but still, we had to read about you saving the vice president and bein' married in the supermarket tabloids while we were out grocery shopping."

"Sorry about that, Pops," Daniel said, shuffling his feet. "I meant to call you guys and explain, but things have been too busy."

"Too busy to give us the good news?"

Sarah whirled around at the sound of the new voice. The rear door of the blue minivan was already open, and the ramp extended as another person rolled out, stopping inches from her. "You must be Sarah," the man in the motorized wheelchair said, his teeth white against his tanned skin. "I'm Thomas Rogers, Daniel's dad."

"Nice to meet you, Thomas" she said, taking the hand offered to her.

"And that's my mate, Beau, Daniel's other dad." Thomas chuckled as he cocked his head at Stetson man. "From the look on your face, I'm guessing my son hasn't told you anything about us." He raised a brow at Daniel.

"Not intentionally," he said defensively.

"I hope they're good reasons, son," Beau said.

"I'll explain everything to you guys, I promise. But first, you should know, she's my mate too," Daniel added. "And we just bonded."

A wide smile broke across Thomas's face. "Mates? That's fantastic."

Beau slapped him on the shoulder. "Congratulations, son. I told you, you were gonna find your mate one day."

"What's going on?" Adam asked as he rolled toward them.

"Pops, Dad," Daniel began. "This is Adam, Sarah's brother. Adam, these are my dads."

"What's up?" Adam asked.

"Nice to meet you, son," Beau said, walking over to him and giving him a vigorous handshake.

Thomas reached over and took Adam's hand once Beau let go. "Hello, Adam. Lovely to meet you. I'm glad to see you're making use of our other van."

"Oh cool, thanks for letting me borrow it," he said.

"Come on, let's head inside," Thomas suggested. "And you can tell us about the wedding."

They let Adam and Thomas lead the way, with Beau opening the front door so the two of them could roll up into the house.

Things clicked into place in Sarah's brain as she watched Daniel's parents. The van. The ramps and ground floor bedrooms in the house. The ADA-accessible trails in the mountains. How did she not notice these things?

They went inside, following the trio into the kitchen, stopping at the doorway to give Adam and Thomas room to maneuver. Beau was already rooting around in the fridge.

"I'm sure you have a lot of questions," Daniel whispered to her as he took her hand and threaded his fingers through his. "Beau is my biological dad, and my mom died giving birth to me. They weren't mates, but they loved each other just the same. He was devastated when she died. We moved here from Texas when he got the job as a ranger. He never had a relationship after her because he was busy raising me, at least not for a couple of years. One day, while he was on patrol, he meets this hot-shot lawyer whose car broke down in the mountains."

"That's an amazing story," she said. "They look like they're still so in love." She had seen it in the way the couple had looked each other, and how Beau kept his hand on Thomas's shoulder, or how Thomas's eyes tracked his mate wherever he went. It all made sense now, somehow. Why Daniel was the way he was, knowing these two had raised him.

"What are you two doin' over there, standing around like a pair of lost calves?" Beau called as he put a six-pack on the table. "Git your asses over here and sit down."

"I love what you've done to the house, Daniel," Thomas said as they sat down. "I'm so proud of you."

"Thanks, Dad," Daniel said as he accepted a beer from Beau.

"So, did you know she was your mate right away?" Thomas asked. "Did your grizzly tell you?"

Daniel chuckled. "It sure did. And as you can tell, she couldn't wait to put a ring on it."

"Hey!" she protested, slapping him on the arm. "That's not what happened. Er, at least not from what I can remember."

He smirked at her. "Well, let me tell you what I can remember."

The rest of the night proceeded with much merriment as they ate, drank, told stories, joked, laughed, and let Adam have one sip of beer. Eventually, as the hours passed, Thomas and Beau declared that it was time for them to retire.

Later, when everyone settled into their rooms, Daniel pulled Sarah into the empty living area.

"I like your parents a lot," she confessed. "They're good people."

"And they like you too," he said. "So ..."

She frowned at him. "What's wrong?"

"Well ... I wanted to wait until I got a ring to ask you this but —" He got down on one knee. "Will you marry me, Sarah Mendez?"

"Marry you?" she chuckled. "We're already married, silly.

Aren't we doing this in the wrong order by the way? Getting married, sleeping together, then falling in love?"

"I guess so." He got up and kissed her on the tip of her nose. "Maybe one day, when we're old and gray, we can look longingly at each from our wheelchairs, surrounded by our children, grandchildren, and great-grandchildren, and finally I'll work up enough courage to introduce myself formally and ask you on a real date."

"Be still my heart," she said, rolling her eyes as she placed a hand on her chest. "Well, until that time, how about we just head upstairs and screw like rabbits?"

He chuckled. "Whatever you want, baby doll."

Epilogue

TWO WEEKS LATER ...

The party in the ballroom of the Blackstone Grand Hotel was in full swing with the speakers blaring tunes the DJ played, champagne and food free-flowing, and the dance floor packed with guests. Some people might have called it a wedding reception, but the real wedding that brought together the bride and groom had taken place months ago in a little wedding chapel along The Strip in Las Vegas. However, the happy couple, along with their family and close friends from Blackstone and Nevada, did hop over to the courthouse that morning to have a vow renewal of sorts and exchange rings.

While they would have been happy to have a simple dinner somewhere to celebrate, the dads of the groom insisted on a real wedding reception. "When else am I going to be able to plan something like this?" Thomas had asked. And so, Daniel and Sarah relented.

"Finally," Daniel said when the upbeat tune faded into a slow, romantic song. "I've been waiting all night for this." Rising to his feet, he offered her his hand. "May I dance with my wife, please?"

Sarah, looking absolutely radiant in her short white dress

that made her bronzed skin glow and with her caramel hair down in waves past her shoulders, stood up and took his hand. "Of course."

He led her to the middle of the dance floor, holding her close against his body, marveling at the way they fit each other so perfectly. But then again, everything about them fit perfectly. Brushing a kiss to her cheek, he inhaled her scent. Her arms wound around his neck, and those velvety brown eyes looked up at him with pure love that didn't need to be said out loud, not when it hummed through the bond they shared.

Joy fluttered in his chest, and his grizzly, too, preened with happiness. The mate bond between them grew stronger each day, a fact that brought him and his animal much delight, as well as real contentment.

For most of the song, it was like they were the only two people on the dance floor. But once the song faded to its final notes, the DJ put on a classic jazzy song with a faster rhythm. Though she tried to let go, he only held her close. "One more, please?"

"We can have any many as you want."

"I hope you're ready." He stepped back and took her hand in his, leading her through the steps of an old-fashioned swing dance. Pops had insisted he learned to dance when he was younger, as he thought it was an important skill. She laughed as he spun her around and dipped her low, and applause broke behind them.

"I didn't know you could do that," she said.

"The things you don't know about me might still surprise you," he said.

"Daniel, Sarah!" came an excited voice behind them. It was Darcey, Adam rolling up next to her in his new motorized wheelchair. "That was a great dance set. I didn't even know you were going to do that."

He leaned over and kissed her on the cheek. "Hey, Darce. Are you having fun?"

She nodded, her waves of white blonde hair bobbing around her. "Everyone's been great and ... it's weird being around so many people like me."

"That's great, Darce, and how's the move?"

"One more trip back to Vegas in the morning and we're done," she said.

"Thank God," Adam groaned. "I'm so glad to be out of that town."

"Looking forward to the fall?" Daniel asked. Adam would be attending Lucas Lennox High when school started back, but for now, he was enjoying his summer. They'd all been going up for hikes in the Blackstone Mountains, and next weekend, Daniel would be taking him up on a boy's only camping trip with his parents and a couple of his friends.

"Yeah, yeah," the teen said. "Ugh, can I go back up to the suite now? This party's so boring, and everyone's so old."

Sarah chuckled. "All right. Go on ahead."

"Later," he said and he drove away.

"Go straight to the room!" Sarah called. "And don't even think about going through the mini bar!" But Adam only answered with a dismissive wave.

"Do you want to dance, Darcey?" Daniel asked.

"Um, maybe later?" She wrinkled her nose. "I think ... I think I need to go somewhere ..." Turning on her heel, she dashed off.

Sarah frowned, then shrugged. "She's been acting weird all night."

"I'm sure she's just feeling excited and unnerved being surrounded by all these shifters." Daniel had only met his sister-in-law twice before tonight, and she hadn't told him yet what she was. However, he had detected feathers in her scent, so he suspected she was some kind of avian shifter.

"Congratulations, man." Gabriel had come up behind them, tugging Temperance along. "And great party."

"This place looks amazing," Temperance said as she glanced at the decorations and table settings around them. "I can't believe your dad only needed a couple days to get this all done. Our wedding is months away, and I still don't feel like it's enough time."

"Well, you could get it over with and do what we did," Daniel suggested with a wiggle of his eyebrows.

Temperance's face brightened, "That sounds like a—"

"Nuh-huh," Gabriel said vehemently. "No, we're not going to Vegas. Not that there's anything wrong with that, but my sisters will kill me if we elope."

Temperance pursed her lips. "Then maybe they can do all the planning. And find me a dress, too."

Sarah reached over and patted her on the shoulder. "Still no luck? That local designer can't fit you in?"

"No." Her shoulders dropped as she frowned. "She won't return my calls."

Gabriel snorted. "She must think she's hot shit now, just because she designed gowns for royalty."

"Gabriel," Temperance warned. "Don't say that. I'm sure she's just busy. I'll find another gown, don't worry."

"Anyway," Gabriel continued. "I'm gonna go talk to Damon. He's probably out checking on who's patrolling the perimeter."

Damon had insisted on placing rangers on duty around the reception area just in case The Knights or any media decided to crash the reception.

"I told him extra security wasn't necessary," Daniel said. "Jason says their intelligence hasn't picked up any sign The Knights are sniffing around, and the media's already found their next big story with that celebrity couple and their messy breakup. Tell him and the rest of the guys to come in and join the party."

"All right," Gabriel said. "I think I saw him talking to Krieger out by the gardens."

"And I'll sit with Anna Victoria and J.D.," Temperance said. "Later, guys."

As the other couple walked away, Sarah slipped her hand into his. "Do you really think The Knights won't bother us anymore?"

"I don't think they'll attempt to kidnap me and try to make me hurt anyone," he said. "But I doubt that's the last Blackstone will see of them."

"What about Thoralf? Did he say anything?"

"Not much about his mission," he said. The dragon shifter had left right after The Knights' attack on him, but they kept in touch via text. "He did send me a message this morning, wishing us well and apologizing for not being able to make tonight. He'll drop by for a visit if he's ever passing through."

"Good. I—" Sarah frowned.

"What's wrong?" He sensed his mate's distress through their bond, as did his bear. The grizzly lifted its block head, nostrils flaring. Turning toward where she was looking, he scanned the room for danger. "Did you see any reporters or any suspicious-looking people?"

"No. It's Darcey. I think I see her over there." She brushed passed him, heading toward the exit. He followed her, of course, until they reached her sister, who stood by the doors, her back to them.

"Darce?" She reached over and grabbed the other woman's shoulder and spun her around. "What's the—are you crying?"

Tears streaked down her pale cheeks, which she quickly brushed off. "Nothing," she cried. "It's nothing."

"It's obviously *not* nothing." Sarah gripped both her arms. "What's the matter? Tell me why you're crying."

"Did someone hurt you?" Daniel's voice turned edgy. "Tell me." His grizzly roared at the sight of the female's tears.

"No. Not intentionally," she whispered. "At least I don't think so ... I'm sorry, I have to go. I'm gonna go to my room, I just need to be alone for a bit." Shrugging off Sarah's grasp, she turned and darted toward the elevators.

"Damn it!" Sarah chewed at her lip. "What the hell could have happened? She was fine earlier."

Daniel chewed on his lip. What could have made Darcey cry? Or who? His fingers curled into fists. If he found out who hurt her, he was going rip them into shreds. His inner bear smashed its giant paws together in agreement.

"I know it's our reception," Sarah began. "But Darcey ..."

"She needs you, baby doll. I understand."

"I shouldn't leave you."

"You can come back down after you make sure she's okay," he said then caught her hand, raising it to eye level so they could both look at the gold band encircling her ring finger. "Remember what it says."

Her lips curved up at the corners. "I'll never forget it. I don't think I ever did."

Daniel had recalled her saying something about the chapel on The Strip sending their rings away to be personalized. On his last trip to Vegas to help Sarah and Adam pack up their apartment, he'd swung by, and sure enough, the rings were ready and waiting for them.

"You." He kissed her fingers as he repeated the words engraved inside the gold band and in his heart. "Only you from now on." He could let go just for this moment, because he still had the rest of his life with her. "Let me know how it goes."

Though anxiety still marred her face, she managed a smile. “Love you.”

“Love you too, mate.”

If you want to read a hot, sexy bonus scene from this book just join my newsletter here

http://aliciamontgomeryauthor.com/mailing-list/

You’ll get access to ALL the bonus materials from all my books and my **FREE** novella **The Last Blackstone Dragon.**

The story isn’t done yet.

What—or who—could have made Darcey cry?

Find out by reading **Blackstone Ranger Rogue**

Available at selected online bookstores.

Turn the page for a special preview.

Preview: Blackstone Ranger Rogue

Darcey Wednesday sighed as she watched the happy couple dance to the slow, romantic song playing over the speakers. The ballroom of The Blackstone Grand Hotel was decorated beautifully, setting up a fairy-tale-like background for the bride and groom.

Really, she was ecstatic for Daniel and Sarah. If anyone deserved to live happily ever after, it was her sister. Ever since they met at that god-awful foster home, Sarah had taken care of her and their other adopted sibling, Adam. For over twelve years, Sarah had been like their mother, father, protector, and caregiver all in one. She could have abandoned them when she turned eighteen and was no longer the responsibility of the state, but she didn't. Sarah worked her ass off to get them out of a terrible situation and provide for them all these years.

And now, Sarah had the love of her life, Daniel Rogers, to take care of her. And Darcey would never begrudge her sister happiness.

But that didn't mean she couldn't feel a pang of envy, watching them stare into each other's eyes, holding each other, dancing together. They were two bodies, but one soul. Fated, bonded mates.

Someone jostled her from behind, and she turned her head. It was one of the waiters carrying a tray of champagne as he walked away from her.

A fluttering in her chest distracted her for a moment.

Mine?

She shook her head and smiled sadly.

The fluttering slowed to a weak flapping before it stopped.

Another sigh escaped her lips. She was used to the familiar flutter and the voice in her head. After all, she was a shifter, and for as long as she could remember, had always shared her body with her inner animal. It never bothered her, that she was different. In fact, she wondered what it was like for humans like Sarah and Adam. What was it like to constantly be alone in their thoughts? To not have an inner companion? To not have to struggle to keep it under control?

Yes, most of her life, she'd lived around humans, from the Nevada orphanage where she'd spent the first nine years of her life, to the various foster homes she was shuttled around in until she met Sarah and Adam. Still, it wasn't something she thought about every day—that was just her life. Sure, she'd met a few shifters over the years. When she came close to any of them, she always just *knew* if they were like her. Like a feeling she couldn't describe but a truth she just knew.

Now, here she was, in Blackstone, Colorado, surrounded by other shifters. Hundreds of them. The moment she stepped foot in this town, she knew this place was way different from Las Vegas where she'd lived all her life. Soon, she would be living here full time, too, and opening the first ever brick and mortar shop of Silk, Lace, and Whispers, the online lingerie store she ran with Sarah.

It was exciting, for sure, and she was grateful that Daniel

had invited her to live with them in his house. She and Adam would be occupying two of the bedrooms on the first floor. She would be surrounded by her family—old and new, which included Daniel's parents who she was already growing to love—and would be living in a town where everyone was like *her*.

But she still felt alone. Like there was something out there she was constantly searching for. Like something was missing.

Maybe it was because she wasn't like other shifters here. Her new brother-in-law was a bear, as was his boss, Damon Cooper, whom she met earlier today. His other coworkers in the Blackstone Rangers were wolves, lions, deer, foxes, and of course, she had heard about the Blackstone dragons who protected the town.

But her? She was no apex predator. In fact, she wasn't any kind of predator. Rather, she was the most docile, harmless creature one could imagine—a swan.

She had only been a few days old when she appeared at the doorstep of the St. Margaret Orphanage. The nuns had no idea what she was and had been just as surprised as her when a few years later, she was in the middle of a fight with another kid and *poof*—disappeared under the pile of clothes on the floor. Panicked, she had dashed into the bathroom and saw her reflection in the full-length mirror. She looked like a fluffy gray duck. Yes, as cliched as it sounded—an ugly little duckling. But later on, as she matured, her true form emerged. The ugly duckling turned into a beautiful swan.

Kinda, anyway.

But surely there were other non-predatory shifters around here, right? A raccoon or squirrel, or maybe even other avian shifters?

The music shifted into something more cheerful, jarring her out of her thoughts. Daniel released Sarah and stepped back, then led her into the beginning steps of an old-fashioned swing dance. The crowd cheered and clapped as the couple spun around the dance floor.

"They're so happy, it's disgusting."

Darcey suppressed a smile at the familiar voice. "Disgusting, huh?" she said to her younger brother, Adam, who had popped up beside her in his brand-new motorized wheelchair.

"Yeah." His mouth twisted. "I don't see the big deal with being in love anyway. People can be happy on their own, you know?"

At first, she thought her brother was being his usual sarcastic teen self. But when he looked up at her with those big green eyes, she saw a flash of something that made her heart twitch. It was sympathy.

Aside from the couple themselves, no one was happier about Daniel and Sarah getting together than Adam was. He practically worshiped his new big brother and was thrilled about leaving Nevada to live here. But Adam was not only smart for his sixteen years, but also emotionally mature. She knew he was trying to suppress his happiness because of *her*. He didn't want her to feel bad that Sarah had Daniel, while Darcey remained single.

As far as she knew, Sarah had never dated seriously nor had any long-term boyfriends. In fact, except for two or three guys she'd dated exclusively for a few months and handful of dates over the years, Sarah had been contentedly single, devoting all her time to raising and providing for her and Adam.

She, on the other hand, tended to flit from one relationship to another, with disastrous results. Whenever a guy paid even a modicum of attention on her, she went all in, focusing her time and energy to making the "relationship" work, bending over backward to please him. But none of that mattered because they all ended the same—with her alone and her heart broken.

She was like a big jerk magnet, attracting only the worst men. They seemed nice enough at first, but they more often than not turned into assholes who either ghosted her or stuck around long enough to take advantage of her, whether financially or emotionally. Eventually, she would end up crying and swearing off relationships. But sure enough, a new guy would come along, and well ... her relationship status had more cycles than the Tour de France.

Her swan shook its head sadly.

Mine?

Sure, she could blame it all on her animal side. Weren't swans known for their fidelity, their propensity to mate for life? It seemed like it asked that question—*mine*?—whenever she met a new guy or was near any potential boyfriend. And Darcey was sure each one was "the one," and when it turned out he wasn't, her swan would peck and nag at her to keep looking.

But still, she couldn't help herself. She just wanted to be loved. Was that so bad?

"Sure, people can be content on their own," she said, repeating Adam's words, then placed a hand on his shoulder. "But we can also be happy for them without feeling like we're less for not having what they have." She gave his shoulder a squeeze, then smiled down at him. He smirked back at her in that way only teenagers can, and she chuckled.

Back on the dance floor, the music faded out, and Daniel dipped Sarah low and kissed her, much to the delight of the spectators.

"C'mon," she said. "I haven't talked to them the whole night. Let's go say hi." She hurried past all the other guests, who made way for them as they made a beeline for the couple. "Daniel, Sarah! That was a great dance set. I didn't even know you were going to do that."

Daniel flashed her a smile that reached all the way to his

bright silvery blue eyes. Leaning down, he kissed her on the cheek. "Hey, Darce. Are you having fun?"

That feeling came over her as she sensed his bear. She wasn't frightened or anything. In fact, his animal's presence felt familial and protective. "Everyone's been great and ... it's weird being around so many people like me." He didn't ask about how she felt being surrounded by other shifters, but she could just tell it was on his mind.

"That's great, Darce, and how's the move?"

When he had asked her to come live with them in Blackstone, the choice was easy. She wasn't really attached to Las Vegas, plus, with their online sales skyrocketing, she and Sarah realized they could open their shop here instead of their original plan of starting it in Summerlin, not to mention, quit her old crappy retail job. The day she'd handed in her notice to her awful boss Agnes was one of the happiest in her life. "One more trip back to Vegas in the morning and I'm done." All she had to do was pick up the last of their stuff at their old apartment, hand in the keys to the landlord, and drive back.

"Thank God," Adam groaned. "I'm so glad to be out of that town."

"Looking forward to the fall?" Daniel asked. Adam was set to start school at the local high school, one that Daniel himself had attended.

"Yeah, yeah," the teen said. "Ugh, can I go back up to the suite now? This party's so boring and everyone's so old."

Sarah chuckled. "All right. Go on ahead."

"Later," he said as he drove away.

"Go straight to the room!" Sarah called out. "And don't even think about going through the mini bar!" But Adam only answered with a dismissive wave.

Daniel turned to her. "Do you want to dance, Darcey?"

It was really sweet of him to ask, and she was about to say

yes when the fluttering in her chest came back.

Mine?

"Um, maybe later?" She wrinkled her nose. A strange tingling came over her as her swan beat its wings madly in her chest.

Mine?

"I think ... I think I need to go somewhere ..."

Her feet took her away from the dance floor like they had a life of their own. The flapping of wings inside her was so loud, the noise and music around her faded away. Her swan frantically swung its head side to side as if searching for something. Feeling her swan's frenetic energy, she had no choice but be swept away by its whim, and she dashed across the ballroom, sidestepping other guests.

Mine?

Her vision tunneled, focusing on a pinpoint, leading her toward the bar. There were several people there, but one particular person caught her attention despite the fact that his back was to her and she could only make out dark hair and broad shoulders. Her hand reached out and tapped him on the arm. "Excuse me," she breathed out.

Slowly, he turned around. His dark head was bowed, his gaze going immediately to the exposed cleavage of her low-cut dress. "Hey, sweetheart." A smile spread across his lips as his head slowly tilted up. "What can I do for—"

Mine!

"—you?"

Light golden-brown eyes stared right into her, sending electricity across her skin as she heard something from deep within him answer back: *Mine.*

"Yes," she gasped. "It's me." Her swan squawked animatedly. This was it. It was *him.*

When she heard that Sarah and Daniel were mates, she

almost didn't believe it. Growing up, with no one to explain to her what being a shifter was all about, she could only do her own research on the Internet, and even then, the information was not really accurate or scientific.

But she had heard about mates—that fate paired shifters with someone they were intended to be with and that only those with animals inside them would be able to tell who their mate was.

She mentally slapped her forehead. God, she was so dumb. Her swan was looking, looking, looking all the time. Trying to find him in all those guys she dated. Asking that question —*mine?*—and never getting an answer back because they were all wrong.

But now, he was here. Even though she didn't realize that she was looking for him, she knew it: He was the one she had been searching for.

And, oh dear, he was *breathtaking*. He was tall, a couple of inches over six feet with a lean, graceful build. He wasn't overly hulking like Daniel or many of the shifters here, but his shoulders were broad, and his biceps strained against his shirt. He was handsome, too, with firm lips and a chiseled, clean-shaven jaw, but what she couldn't tear her gaze away from was his eyes. They were the color of molten honey, and she wanted to lose herself in them.

Joy burst through her, making her heart leap out of her chest. She couldn't stop the smile on her face, even if she'd wanted to. Looking up at him, she could see the shock register on his face as his eyes widened and his jaw slackened.

"Yo, Anders!" someone called from behind. "You joining us?"

He didn't answer, just kept staring at her. Darcey couldn't move either. His companion peeked from behind him, said something, then shrugged and walked away.

Time ticked by, with neither of them saying anything or moving. Finally, she managed a breath and lunged forward, wrapping her arms around him. *Oh God, he smelled so good.* "I can't believe it," she whispered. "I didn't think I'd find you."

He tensed in her arms, and something in her brain got through the blissful cloud surrounding her. Frowning, she released him and stepped back. "Your name is Anders? I'm Darcey. Darcey Wednesday. I'm your—"

"I know who you are."

Of course he did. This actually made it easier. Sarah had told her that although Daniel had known instantly she was his mate, she didn't know because she was human, and that had caused some problems between them initially. "Great. So ... do you want to, like, go somewhere to talk? Or you can meet my family?"

His nostrils flared, and his jaw hardened. "No, I don't think so."

Oh God, she sounded stupid. Maybe they were supposed to do something else? "Oh. Okay. What do you want to do, then?"

His Adam's apple bobbed as he swallowed hard. "Listen, Daisy—"

"Darcey," she corrected. Her swan pecked its beak toward him irritably.

"Yeah. Okay. I don't do relationships."

She blinked. "Excuse me?"

The corner of his mouth quirked up. "You seem like a sweet girl, Darla. But I'm not the one for you."

Was he joking? "B-but I heard it. My animal said it. And yours—"

"Be that as it may, this just isn't going to work out, Dolly."

"But we're—"

"I like what I see, though." His voice dipped low, and he lifted his hand, tracing a finger over her arm, up to her shoulder and collarbone, then followed the vee of her dress down her chest.

Warmth spread through her as she closed her eyes, and she bit her lip to keep from moaning when his knuckles brushed the tops of her breasts.

"You're pretty enough, and I'm not picky. Wanna go meet me in the janitor's closet for a quick screw? This party's getting boring anyway."

His words slammed into her, making her eyes snap open. "A-a quick screw? That's what you want?"

"Yeah, sure." He pulled his hand away. "But it won't mean anything. If you're looking for someone to take you on romantic dates and whisper sweet nothings and live happily ever after with, then go find someone else. I prefer my lays with no strings attached."

This wasn't happening. Surely this was some kind of joke. "I … I don't believe you. You don't mean what you're saying." He must have felt it too. She *heard* his animal roar it out. What was he anyway?

A vision flashed in her head. Something big with large teeth and sharp claws. Stripes and fur and—

He let out a sardonic laugh. "I meant every word, sweetheart." The endearment dripped with acid. "If you don't want to get hurt, stay away from me." Turning on his heel, he put the glass in his hand back on the bar and walked away.

She stood there, frozen. Afraid to make a sound. Afraid to make a move. She was still as a statue, calm as a millpond on the outside.

But inside, a storm of emotions churned. Her swan cried out in distress, not knowing what was happening. The only thing it could focus on was that he—their mate—was walking away from them.

Her chest began to ache something fierce. It started small at first, like a tiny hairline crack along the edges of an icy river. But then it began to expand and grow until it felt like something inside her split apart. Tears sprung in her eyes and the only thing she knew right now was that she *had to get out of there.* Before she had a full-on break down.

Somehow, she managed to pry her feet from where they were stuck to the ground and began to walk. One foot in front of the other. No one was paying any mind to her as they laughed and danced and drank like there was nothing wrong in the world. She nearly made it out when she halted right by the exit. Her swan begged her to go back. To find their mate and make him see. Make him listen.

"He doesn't want us," she whispered.

"Darce?" It was Sarah. Her sister's hand landed on her shoulder and spun her around. "What's the—" Sarah sucked in a breath. "Are you crying?"

Her hands automatically brushed the tears spilling down her cheeks. "Nothing," she cried. "It's nothing."

"It's obviously *not* nothing." Sarah's brown eyes blazed as she gripped both her arms. "What's the matter? Tell me why you're crying."

"Did someone hurt you?" Daniel said in a menacing tone. "Tell me."

The outrage from Daniel's inner bear made her jump. She didn't even realize he was right there too. Because of course he was. He would be beside Sarah for the rest of their lives. He would never leave her or tell her to stay away.

"No. Not intentionally," she whispered. How could she even begin to explain it? "At least I don't think so ... I'm sorry, I have to go. I'm gonna go to my room. I just need to be alone for a bit." Shrugging off Sarah's grasp, she turned and sprang toward the elevators. Frantically, she tapped on the call button, waiting for the doors to open and darted inside as soon as the car arrived. However, as the doors were about to close, she saw Sarah running toward her.

"Stop!" Her sister made it just in time to slip her fingers between the doors. Stepping inside, she took Darcey by the shoulders. "Tell me what's wrong."

She shook her head. Her throat burned so bad that she was scared to speak.

"Darce." Sarah's tone was firmer now. "You know I'm going to hound you until you tell me what's wrong. I'm going to stay here and miss my entire reception if I have to, but I won't leave until I find out who hurt you and make them pay. Please."

Slowly, she lifted her head and stared up at her sister's face. They weren't biological sisters, not even close. But they were sisters of the heart, bound together by the vow they made the day they met at that miserable foster home. It was the first time she ever felt real love, and maybe the last.

"Oh, Sarah," she cried, then burst into tears.

"Darce. Oh no." Sarah's arms wound around her. "C'mon, let's go to your room."

Thank goodness Sarah was there, because otherwise, Darcey wouldn't have known how to get back to her room. Once they were inside, her sister sat her down on the bed, got a cold, wet towel from the bathroom and pressed it to her face, all the while soothing her as she cried.

When the tears finally slowed down, Sarah took her hand in hers. "Now tell me what happened."

Sarah always made her feel safe, so Darcey told her everything. Every single, humiliating detail of that short conversation with her mate. It was obvious her sister was outraged, and Darcey would always be grateful for the fact that she had her back all this time.

"Who was it?" Sarah asked.

"I don't know ... never met him before. Though someone

called him Anders."

Sarah's face completely changed from sympathetic to pure, deep anger. "A-Anders? Anders Stevens is your *mate*?"

She sniffed. "I didn't get his last name. But how many Anders could there be?"

Her sister shot to her feet, hands fisting at her sides. "For his sake, it better be another Anders who made you cry." She bared her teeth. "I don't care if he's Daniel's friend or that he can turn into a tiger, I'm going to kill that motherfucker!"

"Sarah, no!" Her inner swan protested too. "I mean ... please don't make a big deal—"

"Not a big deal?" she said incredulously. "Saying all those things to you ... even if he wasn't your mate, I would still kick his ass."

"Sarah ..." Grabbing her arm, she dragged her sister back down next to her. "Please ... I just want to forget this night ever happened."

"Oh, sweetie ..." Sarah put an arm around her and pulled her close. "It'll be all right. You'll be all right."

Would she? But instead of saying that, she nodded. "You're right. Just ... just don't tell anyone, okay?"

Sarah hesitated. "I won't tell just anyone. But Daniel ... I can't keep this from him."

"I ..." She bit her lip. Sarah was right, of course. Daniel was her mate. If she kept things from him, he would probably be hurt. "All right, but he won't tell anyone else, right? Not even Adam?"

"No, he won't, I promise."

She let out a relieved sigh, though the tightness in her chest did not go away. "Thank you, Sarah. For being here."

"Of course. I love you, Darce. I'll be here for you anytime."

Slumping over, she buried her face in Sarah's shoulder. "Love you, too, Sarah."

Printed in the USA
CPSIA information can be obtained
at www.ICGtesting.com
LVHW041115210923
758623LV00002B/290

9 781952 333200